As If It Was Real

Beca Lewis

Perception Publishing

Copyright ©2023 by Beca Lewis

All rights reserved.

No portion of this book may be reproduced in any form without written permission from the publisher or author, except as permitted by U.S. copyright law.

Contents

	Prologue	1
1.	One	3
2.	Two	6
3.	Three	11
4.	Four	16
5.	Five	20
6.	Six	24
7.	Seven	28
8.	Eight	32
9.	Nine	37
10.	Ten	41
11.	Eleven	45

12.	Twelve	50
13.	Thirteen	54
14.	Fourteen	59
15.	Fifteen	64
16.	Sixteen	69
17.	Seventeen	74
18.	Eighteen	78
19.	Nineteen	82
20.	Twenty	86
21.	Twenty-One	90
22.	Twenty-Two	94
23.	Twenty-Three	98
24.	Twenty-Four	102
25.	Twenty-Five	107
26.	Twenty-Six	112
27.	Twenty-Seven	116
28.	Twenty-Eight	120
29.	Twenty-Nine	125
30.	Thirty	130
31.	Thirty-One	134

32.	Thirty-Two	139
33.	Thirty-Three	143
34.	Thirty-Four	148
35.	Thirty-Five	152
36.	Thirty-Six	156
37.	Thirty-Seven	160
38.	Thirty-Eight	163
39.	Thirty-Nine	167
40.	Forty	171
41.	Forty-One	176
42.	Forty-Two	181
43.	Forty-Three	186
44.	Forty-Four	190
45.	Forty-Five	194
46.	Forty-Six	198
47.	Forty-Seven	202
48.	Forty-EIght	207
49.	Forty-Nine	211
50.	Fifty	216
51.	Fifty-One	220

52. Fifty-Two	224
53. Fifty-Three	228
54. Fifty-Four	233
55. Fifty-Five	237
56. Fifty-Six	242
57. Fifty-Seven	246
58. Fifty-Eight	249
Author Note	252
Acknowledgements	254
Also By Beca	256
About Beca	258

Prologue

Daniel Jacobs stared at his father's paintings in wonder. How had he missed what a beautiful artist his father had been?

I suppose if I would have stayed home, I would have known, Daniel thought. *Perhaps then I could have helped him, if he would have let me.*

Instead, Daniel had traveled the world looking for adventure, trying to escape his father's abusive nature. Maybe if he had seen his father's art, he would have discovered this hidden part of his father. One that saw such beauty and had such skill to bring it to life.

It turned out that his father was a mystery. Daniel thought he had known his father well—a cruel man to his wife and son, both of whom he had abandoned to concentrate on his art.

But everything he knew about his father had to be partially a lie. How could a man like his father paint like this? What had he missed about him? And now that his father was dead, would he ever find out what was real about his father and what had been a lie?

Daniel shook his head, his mind swirling with unanswered questions. The man who had never shied away from conflict, who wielded an indomitable influence over others, who navigated life with reckless abandon, had ended his own existence, all the while he was crafting these magnificent works of art.

Perhaps, Daniel mused, he had never truly known his father at all.

One

Cindy Lee Jones sat in the corner of the room, knees pulled up to her chest, and let herself wallow in her misery. Her unhappiness was deep and unyielding. She tried to picture how she felt as a color and failed. Black wouldn't be deep enough. Maybe a muddy, ugly brown. No. Not even that.

And that she was thinking about her misery as a color made it even worse. She thought like an artist. Why wasn't she one?

Surveying the room, she saw the fruits of her labor, a testament to her wretchedness. Paintings were piled two or three deep against every wall, leaving only the doorway and window unburdened. The turned away canvases seemed to accuse her, whispering that someone else could have imbued them with greatness, something she could never achieve.

She had tried. How she had tried. The evidence lay before her, paintings not even worth a second glance. The idea of ever feeling pride or satisfaction seemed distant, almost impossible. Part of her yearned to destroy them, to slice through each canvas like a wrist, letting paint bleed in place of blood.

Even the large canvas on the easel was a disaster. An attempt at something different, only to result in another failure—a reflection of herself. It was time, Cindy thought, to admit she was not an artist and to seek an alternative path. But such thoughts only anchored her further into the room's dark corner.

Despite dedicating her life to the craft, traveling to study with masters and practicing daily, she had gained nothing but a keen eye for great art. It was this critical eye that fueled the success of her art gallery. But it also shattered her illusions of being an artist.

It felt so unfair. She adored the process of painting—the scents, the colors, the surprises that emerged on the canvas. But the disappointment was too much to bear. The dream of being a great artist seemed destined to be abandoned, leaving her to find solace in her gallery and her friends.

However, this realization only deepened her sadness. Everyone around her was finding happiness, while she was left feeling jealous and ignored. Her role was that of a helper, never the one at the center of the story.

April was moving forward with her dream of designing homes, and slowly looking more like herself now that her serial killer husband, Ron Page, had died.

Marsha was exploring the freedom of being herself both by continuing her relationship with Nicky and creating a dance and theatre studio in the house Ron had given April.

Bree and Booker had stopped pretending they were just friends, and Bree looked as happy as she had ever looked. All of Bree's secrets were out in the open now. Besides, Bree had her daughter, Mary, and her daughter's family—baby Rho and husband Seth. Their story was like a fairy tale. Hard at first, then happily ever after.

Cindy thought that Judith and Bruce were also moving closer to declaring themselves a couple, even though everyone knew that they already were.

And even though Cindy was happy for all of them, she knew that the feeling deep inside her was one of jealousy. She was now the odd woman out, and no one seemed to notice. Instead, she was someone people counted on when they needed her, but never, ever, someone in her own right. And definitely not an artist. She had no choice but to accept her fate.

It looked like being helpful to other people was going to be her legacy, and Cindy knew she had to accept that as enough for her. Because at the moment, she didn't have a choice in the matter. This was all she was going to get.

Cindy struggled to her feet, leaning on the wall for support. It was time for a change. It was time to take care of herself. It used to be she could just stand up. Now she had to practically be a contortionist just to get to her feet.

She knew Marsha was teaching a class called chair yoga. Maybe it was time to take it. *How many times does it take for you to notice what needs to be done and then do it?* Cindy asked herself. For others, just once. For herself, not so much.

Well, that changes now, Cindy said, brushing herself off as she walked to the door. She put her paintbrushes down on the table, turned off the light, and shut the door. She'd send someone in someday to clean up the room and get rid of every trace of art in it. Maybe turn it into a guest room. It was time to move on.

And although she didn't enter the room again for a long time, having given up on her dream of being an artist, she never did get around to having the room cleaned up either.

Because, as fate would have it, Cindy's life was about to change in ways even she could not have imagined.

Two

"I don't know what to do about her," Marsha said to April.

April knew who Marsha was talking about. Since the girl had started taking dance classes with Marsha, that's all Marsha seemed to talk about. The new girl.

Marsha and April were having Sunday brunch in the newly installed upstairs kitchen, with its handcrafted cabinets and granite countertops. It was small but beautiful, every appliance thoughtfully placed where it could be used but not always seen.

After Ron died, they had changed the plans of the Ruby House. Ron had wanted elegance and grandeur, but Marsha and April wanted something comforting and effortless. They had both lost someone they loved, and that had changed them. Who they wanted to be in the world now was something they were discovering together.

Although April's husband, Ron Page, had turned out to be an evil man, that didn't change the fact that for over thirty years, April had loved him. She mourned both the passing of her husband and the father of her children, not the man she found out he had been.

Marsha had lost her father. This time for good. Not knowing who he was her whole life, she had thought he was dead. But then she met her father, Harry, and she learned he had watched over her all her life.

Harry's death, after only knowing him for a few days, threw everything Marsha knew about herself up into the air, and it was only now settling. Marsha mourned both the man, and like April, the life they could have had together if secrets hadn't kept them apart.

While only half listening to Marsha talk about the new girl—she'd heard it all before—April glanced around the kitchen. From where she sat, she could see the hallway. On one side of the hallway was the door to her master bedroom with its own bath and small office space. On the other side of the hallway, facing the back garden, was the same arrangement for Marsha.

At the end of the hall was another bedroom with its own bath. It was meant to be a guest room, and April prayed that someday her children would be willing to come visit. They were still reeling from the discovery of who their father had been and blaming April for not knowing.

For April, it was double the pain. She lost the man she thought she knew and her children at the same time. She sighed and turned her thoughts to how much the house had changed and what it meant to her.

Downstairs was a large studio with sliding doors that could turn the large room into small rooms when needed. At one end of the studio, they could lift the floor a few feet to make a stage. A dressing room and two bathrooms were now where the dining room and kitchen used to be.

An office for the studio and her new design business jutted out from the front of the house. Seth had worked his magic, and it looked as if it had always been there. With a mini refrigerator and a coffee machine, it had everything they needed to meet with clients and students.

April loved every part of the downstairs with its constant influx of students and sometimes a client for her, but mostly she loved that the upstairs was a private space just for her and Marsha.

The kitchen was common ground, and it was where some of their best discussions took place. Instead of a dining table, they had a booth big enough for six, and a board that slid out at the end to accommodate even more people when all the Ruby Sisters and their friends came over.

Instead of a wall, there was a window that looked out onto the backyard garden and the newly installed large deck. The backyard and deck were Marsha's favorite places in the house.

Sometimes Marsha took her classes out to the deck to practice. "Being outside changes everything," she would tell them. "Let nature teach you how to dance."

At first, her students didn't understand, but some of them were feeling the difference it made to dance under the trees. Marsha also taught morning yoga on the deck and planned to stay out there until it became too cold.

Across from the booth, on the other side of the kitchen, there was another large picture window. The red maple tree that lived in the front yard took up some of the view, but they could still see the driveway to the house, and in the winter, when the leaves were gone, they could see almost all of Main Street. To both of them, it felt as if they had a pulse on the town, while keeping their lives as private as possible.

April brought her attention back to Marsha, who had stopped talking and was waiting for April to focus on her.

"I'm sorry," April said, "Daydreaming."

Both of them knew it was more than that. And Marsha understood. She did the same thing sometimes—drifted off thinking about something else—or just not thinking at all. Two wounded souls finding their feet again. The perfect pair of friends.

Still, she was anxious about the new girl, Emma Drake, so when April asked, "What did she do this time?" Marsha was happy to tell her. Maybe April could come up with a solution to help her.

Not that Emma wanted help. Emma made it abundantly clear that Marsha was to stay out of her life. She was only in dance class because her mother made her come. She claimed to hate it.

And Marsha could leave it at that, except Emma had talent and loved to dance, which is why she had waived Emma's fees when her mother explained their situation. Because despite everything she did to pretend that she didn't like to dance, to Marsha's discerning eye, it was crystal clear that Emma was lying to herself and everyone else.

But it wasn't just her talent that had caught Marsha's eye. It was that Emma was troubled. Something was going on that made her act out. She constantly disrupted the class, alternating between loud or sullen. The rest of the class was suffering from her behavior, and Marsha knew she should tell her she wasn't welcome there anymore.

And why she hadn't done that yet was what she wanted to talk over with April. The girl was hurting. She and April were still hurting. Maybe they were the ones who could discover what was going on, and then help Emma.

The Ruby Sisters had pulled each other out of one problem or another all of their lives. What would they have done if they hadn't had each other? Especially this past year. It was a year from hell, and at the same time, because they had each other—it had overflowed with love and grace.

Maybe they could do the same for Emma and her mother, Veronica. Because even though it was the girl Marsha was talking about, it was Emma's mother who had really caught her eye. Because although Emma's mother looked as if she was doing fine—always well-dressed, polite, and smiling—Marsha knew the signs. Something was wrong. And although it was Emma doing the acting out, it was only because her mother wasn't.

Three

"Are you sure this is going to be okay with your mother?" Daniel asked Robert for what seemed like the tenth time in the past week.

And Robert answered the same way each time. "She'll be ecstatic that I am coming to visit."

"You know, you never say that she'll be happy that you are bringing a friend, and you know that's what I am really asking. It's because you're not sure you should bring me, isn't it? Maybe that's why you wrote a letter instead of texting her or calling her. You didn't want to hear her say no."

Robert looked over at his friend and realized he would not stop asking until he told him the reason he had written. Daniel was a questioner. Never satisfied until he found out an answer to a puzzle.

He and Daniel had met ten years before on a train traveling across Europe. Robert couldn't even remember where the train was going or why he had been on it. Too many trips to remember all of them.

At the time Robert had been traveling with his current boyfriend, he didn't remember who it had been. All he remembered was that he had become bored and went looking for someone to talk to. He'd gone to the dining car, figuring someone had to be there.

He saw Daniel right away. He was hard to overlook. Robert judged him to be about ten years older than himself, tall, dark, and good-looking. Daniel had been sitting at a table by himself with an Ansel Adams book of photography open in front of him, which he was staring at mindlessly as he ate his sandwich.

Stopping at the table, Robert had said, "How did he capture the essence of that place just using black and white?"

Startled, Daniel had looked up, and then gestured for Robert to sit down with him. The conversation they had that day lasted for hours and continued through the rest of the train trip.

Robert's friend had gotten off at the next train stop once he realized Robert was no longer interested in him. But it wasn't because Daniel was gay. He wasn't. It was because Robert had discovered that with Daniel, he could have conversations about ideas, and he was no longer bored.

Daniel was on the train because his heart was heavy with the tension from a strained meeting with his father at his art studio. The encounter had left him emotionally drained, so he opted for a spontaneous journey to clear his thoughts. The rhythmic motion of the train promised solace, providing Daniel the space he needed before eventually returning to his life in New York City, where he taught photography and occasionally sold his captivating images.

For the rest of that train ride, Robert and Daniel discussed many things. They both had an eclectic view of the world. Not the same one, but that helped to make their discussions more lively. However, they had many things in common, one of which was that they both enjoyed living a slightly untethered vagabond life.

After that trip, they went their separate ways but kept in touch through Facebook and Twitter. However, they hadn't seen each other again until a few weeks ago, once again by chance., this time in New York City. Although New York was Daniel's home, Robert had only vaguely remembered that fact. He was passing through, as usual.

However, this time Robert wasn't traveling for work. After learning the truth about his father, the desire to write anything, or to be with anyone, had dried up. He had some money saved up and was then just roaming around, looking for himself, he supposed.

So when Robert stopped in to a small coffee shop and saw a man sitting in the back of the room with a book spread in front of him, he thought of Daniel. But even then, it took him a moment to realize it really was his friend. Robert knew everyone aged, but Daniel had really changed.

Yes, he was still tall and lean, but now his hair was turning gray, and he had bags under his eyes. But it was the sadness that stood out.

Robert walked over to the table, coffee in hand, and, glancing at the book, asked, "Still reading books while you eat?"

Daniel looked up, his face grim. But when he realized it was Robert standing in front of him, his dark blue eyes lit up, and he smiled as he stood to hug him.

"My God, man. What are you doing here?" Daniel asked.

Robert took one look at Daniel and thought that some kind of divine direction must have brought him there.

"I think I might have been looking for you without realizing it."

Daniel felt a well of emotion rising, and afraid he might break down, gestured to the seat in front of him, and simply said, "And I am grateful that you found me."

Once again, they talked for hours. This time, about what they had been doing the past ten years, and their fathers, and how they never knew them.

They went to lunch together, and when Daniel discovered Robert was staying at a grungy hotel, invited him to stay at his flat. Robert took him up on it—not just for him, but for Daniel, who Robert suspected needed a little looking after. Daniel had always been a loner, but this time, Robert knew Daniel had become lonely.

Now, a few weeks later, Robert had grown restless. Besides, he knew it was time he grew up enough to go see his mother, so he asked Daniel to take a trip to Spring Falls with him.

"Why?" Daniel had asked.

"I need to go see my mother. I have never been to the town where she lives, but she says it's pretty. Small, but apparently charming and full of interesting people."

"To your mother."

"Well, I think it might be true. Four friends of hers she's known since elementary school are all now living in Spring Falls and now my mom has a business designing spaces. One of her friends runs a dance theatre school out of the house mom owns. Another one of her friends runs an art gallery, and one is a rather famous author. And the other friend seems to know everyone in town and helps mom with her business.

"Strangely, I have met none of them. My father kept my mom away from her friends, and we had only visited once when I was a baby. But mom tells me about them all the time. I know she wouldn't have survived without them.

"I feel as if I need to thank them all and apologize to my mother for running out on her when she needed me the most."

Daniel had mostly tuned out, thinking the last thing he needed was to see people, but when Robert mentioned that one of his mother's friends owned an art gallery, he had perked up. Maybe they'd show his photographs. And he still needed to deal with his father's paintings, and he didn't want to do that in New York, where everyone knew his father, Cedric Jacobs.

So he had said yes to going. But he was worried about why Robert had written instead of called. What if Robert was afraid of bringing him? So he asked again, "Why the letter?"

Robert threw his hands up in exasperation.

"Okay, I give up. I wrote to her because she's been begging me to come visit, so I know she will be ecstatic, and she loves meeting new people. So it's not about you. It's about me. In all the messages I have sent her, I didn't tell her I had returned to the states, so I thought it would be easier to tell her in a letter, than hearing her get upset with me on the phone."

Daniel stared at his younger friend and wondered if he was telling the whole truth. Something was still wrong, but he had to assume that it had nothing to do with him. Probably it was about Robert's father. And Daniel understood that. They both had fathers they thought were one thing, and then turned out to be something completely different.

The distinction between the two was that Robert had already discovered his father's identity and had time to process his feelings about it. On the other hand, Daniel was only beginning to unearth the truth about his own father. Despite the mutual dislike between them, Daniel felt compelled to seek answers. He needed to unravel the mystery behind the paintings and understand the reasons behind his father's tragic decision to take his own life.

He didn't expect the answer to be in Spring Falls, but going there might clear his head.

"Ready?" Robert asked, zipping his suitcase.

Taking a deep breath, Daniel answered that he was and realized he was looking forward to it. Something needed to change in his life. Maybe Spring Falls would provide the impetus for that to happen.

Four

Judith arrived at the coffee shop earlier than usual in anticipation of their Monday morning ritual. Cindy was a punctual person, but Judith enjoyed being the first to arrive anywhere.

Besides, this way it ensured that they would get their cherished table, nestled in a secluded corner yet offering a sweeping view of the bustling room. Judith could also observe the comings and goings through the expansive plate-glass window. This prime spot provided the perfect vantage point for their lively conversations and people-watching adventures.

Judith also enjoyed having her first cup of coffee alone, the hum and bustle of people around her a white noise. Everyone knew her, but they also knew that this was not the time to talk to her. Just nod and smile, and Judith would nod and smile back, her mind traveling through ideas and thoughts like a car rushing down a freeway.

On this day, her mind was blissfully free of any pressing concerns or looming worries. Sure, there were a few clients that required extra attention, but no one was in dire straits. As late summer unfurled its languid embrace, an air of carefree relaxation enveloped everyone around her, including herself. It was a time when the world seemed to slow down, encouraging her to relish each moment, savoring the fleeting warmth and sunlight before autumn's arrival.

She and Bruce were planning a getaway. Well, she wasn't planning it. Bruce was doing all the work, and she was happy to let him do it. If she could pass off a decision to someone she trusted, she would, and she definitely trusted Bruce.

They had been through so much together in such a short time, but he had always been there for her and the Ruby Sisters. Judith knew that Bruce's clients trusted him, too. Bruce was slowly building his estate planning practice, choosing his clients carefully. His intention was to keep it small and leave plenty of time for enjoying life.

Judith had similar plans, but she doubted she would keep them. Instead, what she would do was look for interns from the community college, and see if she could train a few of them to become bookkeepers, and maybe lead them into the accounting field. That way, she'd have people she trained to take over even more of her accounting practice. She enjoyed overseeing people and watching them thrive.

That was something she could not give up, even if she wanted to. That, and fixing problems. But since Ron had died, the problem of Ron had died with him. Although other people were working on uncovering all his past crimes, that was no longer the Ruby Sisters problem. They had all stepped away from Ron and his history to concentrate on helping April recover.

So even though she could deny it, Judith knew what she was doing was searching for a new mystery or problem that she could have a hand in solving. And since there wasn't one at the moment, she was willing to take a trip. Who knew? Maybe she'd unearth something while traveling.

Or you could just relax, Judith said to herself. And then laughed. Solving problems was relaxing to her.

The door chimed as Cindy came in. Waving at Judith, she headed to the counter to place her order. Judith held up a small bag to let Cindy know that she had brought cinnamon buns, and Cindy responded with a smile and a thumbs up.

But Judith, always looking for what wasn't working so she could fix it, saw the tremor behind the smile, and noticed a slight slump in Cindy's shoulders she simultaneously felt both worried and grateful.

And being Judith, she felt no guilt over the contrast because now she had someone to help, and since that someone was one of her best friends, it would be even more pleasurable.

Besides, Judith knew she wasn't the cause of the problem. Yes, if that had been the case, she would feel terrible. But she was sure she wasn't, so she was relieved of that responsibility.

But what worried her a little was the question she asked herself. *What if this problem had been there all along, and all of them had been too busy with their lives to notice it?*

Well, she wasn't too busy now. She had noticed. And Cindy was going to tell her what was up eventually and together they would find a solution. They always had. What Judith really loved about the prospect of helping Cindy was that she knew that the solution would reveal itself in unexpected ways, as it always had, and she trusted that it always would.

So when Cindy took a seat smiling as if nothing was up, Judith smiled right back and asked the question she always asked. How was Cindy's art gallery doing? After all, she supplied both the bookkeeper and accountant for most of the businesses in town, including Cindy's, so she had to check on that first.

When Cindy said that all was well, they moved on to other subjects like gardening, the last time they saw baby Rho and how adorable she was becoming, the Ruby House, and planning their next Ruby Sister's bi-monthly night together.

Although they saw each other much more often than that, it wasn't always all together at the same time. Having a regular meeting planned, you can't get out of it, meetings kept them in touch as a group.

As they talked, Judith watched Cindy like a hawk, but there was nothing to see. Because Cindy knew that Judith had detected something going on with her and used every bit of energy she had to mask it. Although the Ruby Sisters had agreed to not keep secrets, Cindy felt that this was not a secret that would hurt anyone, so it didn't need to be shared.

It didn't matter that she would quit trying to be an artist. Instead, she would devote her time and energy to the art gallery, and maybe, just maybe, take better care of herself. Perhaps she'd even try teaching art. What was that saying, those that can't do, teach? Cindy knew Bruce had taught a class at the community college. Maybe he could get her a position there. Or even easier, she could teach art classes at the gallery.

That thought lit up Cindy's face, so when Judith asked her what she was thinking, she was willing to share her new idea. Judith thought it was a brilliant plan and asked when did Cindy want to start. So, for the rest of their Monday morning coffee, the two of them discussed what teaching art at the gallery might look like.

Neither one of them knew they had just planted a seed that would uncover the mystery that Judith had wished for, while, at the same time, make Cindy's problems worse before they became better.

Five

Emma Drake took one look at her mother and stormed off into her room, slamming the door so hard books on her bookshelf fell onto the floor. She knew the signs. Her mother was in one of her moods, and nothing good would come of staying in the house with her.

In Emma's world, nothing was certain. The shifting moods of her mother were as unpredictable as the wind, leaving her constantly bracing for change. It hadn't always been like this. There was a time when her mother's presence was a reliable anchor amidst the chaos; as they moved from place to place so frequently that their past homes would become a blur. Emma yearned for more stability.

Their constant moving was why she didn't go to school. Why go, when every few months they'd be off again? And even though her mother promised they would stay in Spring Falls forever, that this was now their permanent home, Emma didn't believe her.

Besides, what difference did it make to her now? She could have been like other people who had friends their whole lives. But that would never be true now. The only person she had known her whole life was her mother. And that wasn't saying much since she barely knew her anymore.

Her mother told her to stop whining about it, and start making new friends. But how? Everyone in Spring Falls already had friends and she would never be part of their stupid cliques anyway. She'd discovered that in dance class. Marsha was nice enough, but the kids in class had dissed her, as she knew they would.

No, she mused. She didn't fit in here. But that was fine. All she had to do was endure three more years of homeschooling, and then she'd spread her wings, soaring into a future of her own making. The allure of untamed adventures, yet to be discovered, danced in her imagination. The excitement of the unknown beckoned, promising a life that was entirely hers to shape and explore.

Emma cherished her innate sense of curiosity, viewing it as a precious gift. Yet, her mother found Emma's relentless desire to comprehend the world around her more of an irritation than a virtue. This struck Emma as peculiar, given that her mother had once been an inquisitive soul herself, encouraging Emma to question the "why" behind things. However, everything had shifted a few months ago, and now it felt as if life was constantly trying to crush her spirit.

Emma held onto the hope that someday she would either discover a place where her thirst for knowledge was embraced and celebrated, or her mother would revert to the passionate, curious woman she once was.

For now, though, she needed to be out of the house and go on a small adventure. Picking up the books that had fallen, she apologized to them and put them back up on the shelf. She didn't have many books, but she loved the ones that she took along as they moved from place to place. She had learned that it didn't do any good to have many things. She just had to pack them up every few months.

Except for what was on the shelf, she kept all her other belongings in plastic storage boxes. Her mother kept trying to get her to put her clothes in the dresser and closet, but she refused. She knew her mother. At any moment she might say, "Let's go."

Emma paused for a moment, reminding herself that her mother had never promised they'd stay somewhere before. That was new. Also new was her mother saying that she needed to find a job. Somehow, they always had money. They never had a lot, but always enough that her mom never worked.

A few months ago, that had changed. Now, money was an issue. More than an issue. Something frightening. Why, Emma didn't know. It was just another secret her mother kept from her, and probably what was causing her mother's bad moods.

Emma thought that her mother getting a job would be a good thing. Get her out of the house, maybe make a few friends. Put down roots so that it would be harder to leave. Because even though Emma didn't want to like Spring Falls, she did. Friends or not, she liked the town. Enough to want to stay for a few more years, anyway.

Emma pulled one of the plastic boxes out from under the bed and grabbed her running shoes, fanny pack, and hat. She pushed her hair through the pony tail hole in the back, snapped on the fanny pack, added her phone and keys to it, and laced up her old running shoes. If she wanted new ones, Emma knew she would need to get a job herself to buy them.

As she went to open her bedroom door, Emma couldn't help but glimpse her reflection. Whoever had lived in the room before her had stuck a bunch of square mirrors on the wall by the door, so when she looked at herself, she never saw a whole person, but only bits and pieces.

She thought that was exactly who she was, a person made up of bits and pieces, trying to fit it all together and failing. Lots of cracks and spaces with nothing there. The image fit her perfectly.

Her life was a mosaic, crafted from a myriad of fragments. She possessed a deep-seated passion, a calling that seemed unattainable, so she locked it away within her heart. Inherited from her mother, her tall and slender frame was ideal for ballet, as her mother often reminded her.

Ballet was enjoyable, but she couldn't reveal her true feelings for what she really wanted to do, for fear that it might be snatched away, like so many things in her life. And so, she protected herself from experiencing the familiar sting of loss, by holding her passions close and hidden.

Running was the only thing that felt as if it belonged just to her. Probably because she was by herself, but also because she liked the freedom of being able to go somewhere on her own power.

Emma and her mother, Veronica, lived just off Main Street in a house so small it looked as if it had been put on the lot by mistake. But that kept the rent low, her mother said. Emma liked it because it was so small. It didn't take up space.

It was what she was trying to do. If she didn't take up space, no one would notice her. Except everyone did, because all she did was take up space with her acting out. Emma wished she could stop it. She knew better.

As Emma passed her mother's room, she saw her lying on her bed, eyes closed, and a cold pack on her forehead. *Another migraine,* Emma thought. They made the perfect excuse for her mother to disappear.

She won't even know I am gone, Emma thought, and slipped out the front door, and waited a beat. When she didn't hear her mother's voice, she breathed out in relief. She was free.

Six

Emma took a deep breath and let the clean autumn air fill her body. She did a few stretches and started off towards the woods. It was a few miles away, an easy run. It was early morning, very few people would be around, so she took the route that took her through the small downtown.

Reaching Main Street she looked to her left and could see the large house with the beautiful maple tree in front where she took dance lessons. There was a light on in one of the upper windows, and Emma wondered if her dance teacher and the other woman that lived there could see her standing at the corner.

She almost waved and then stopped herself. What was she thinking? She didn't want to be seen. Turning right on Main, Emma passed the coffee shop, and saw the red-haired woman sitting in the back corner and wondered why she saw that woman everywhere.

Emma knew the woman was a friend of her dance teacher, but who was she? Why was she everywhere? Something about her was both frightening and comforting. When the woman turned her head towards the window, Emma looked away and ran faster.

As she ran, Emma felt the air flow past her, listened to the rhythm of her feet hitting the pavement, and pretended that with each breath out, all the bad thoughts she had flowed away into the wind. With each in breath, she felt lighter and lighter, almost like a puff of dandelion fluff. She knew the feeling wouldn't last forever, but it was good enough for now.

A few blocks down, at the art gallery, Emma ran in place for a moment to look in the window and felt the familiar pull to go inside. But it was closed. And she couldn't go in, anyway. What excuse could she make for being there?

Just outside of town, she passed the entrance to the community college with its huge stone pillars flanking the wide sidewalk that led up to the main building. The campus was so small it could almost pass for a big high school, but she loved the look of it, with its tall spreading trees and benches where she would often see students sitting and reading.

It was another place that pulled her. Maybe she could find a class that she could take. In college, she would be a new student just like everyone else, and maybe there she'd find a friend or two. Emma made a note to herself to go online and find the requirements for her to attend. There was no need to tell her mother. She did most of her classes on her own, anyway.

Thirty minutes later, Emma arrived at the trailhead parking lot. Typically, it would be empty at this time of the day, so it surprised her to see a car already parked there. As she continued running, she reached for her spring-loaded baton from her fanny pack, ensuring that her pepper spray was still clipped to it. Emma kept the baton and spray handy as a precaution against aggressive dogs, a constant concern when running solo.

As she stepped onto the trail, she pulled her energy in so she would disturb the animals and birds as little as possible. This was their place. She was only a visitor. She wondered what it would be like to have a place the same way the forest creatures did. A place they knew through generations. She'd never have that.

Staying alert, Emma ran lightly down the trail, keeping an eye out for whoever belonged to the car in the lot. In the spring, because it was full of the winter melt and spring rains, she could hear the falls almost immediately after entering the woods. Today they were a small murmur, so they didn't hide the sound of someone talking.

Emma stopped running and stepped into the forest by the path. Walking quietly, she followed the curve of the path. She wasn't afraid. The birds were still singing, so they accepted whoever was there.

Peaking around a tree, she saw a woman sitting on the bench close to the falls. She appeared to be talking to the chickadees that were eating seeds out of her hands. Emma smiled at the sight. She had tried doing that but failed. Maybe the birds didn't know her well enough.

The decision to go back or go forward was made for her when the woman turned in her direction and said, "Come on out, I won't bite, and you can help me feed these birds."

Taking a deep breath, Emma stepped back onto the path. She'd seen this woman before, too. She had been at the Ruby House talking to Marsha.

The birds scattered as Emma came forward, and the woman patted the seat beside her.

"Hi, Emma. Marsha pointed you out to me when I was there. I'm Bree Mann."

Bree smiled at the girl, thinking she looked like a deer with her long legs and dark hair pulled back into a ponytail. Skittish like one too.

Emma stared, wondering what to do, but then she saw one of her favorite books sitting on the bench beside Bree and said, "That's one of my favorite books."

"Mine too," Bree said. "Why is it yours?"

Without thinking about it, Emma slid onto the park bench, picked up the book and told the woman why. And for the first time in many months, she was listened to as if she was someone who mattered.

Seven

April made herself another cup of coffee, put the letter on the table, and settled back into the booth. She touched the letter with the tips of her fingers, hoping that some sense of what was in it would come through, but all she felt was worry. Sighing, she turned to look out the window at the garden and then down at Marsha teaching her yoga class on the deck.

It would soon be too cold to be out there. Even today, they all had sweaters on, and a few yellow and red leaves floated down on them, the first signs of fall. But she knew they'd stay out as long as they could.

I should do that with them, April said out loud to herself. *Be a doer, not just an observer.* After all, Marsha had asked her many times to come to class. It would be so easy. It was Monday, a good time to begin a new habit. There was nothing to do but get herself downstairs. But she couldn't bring herself to do it, no matter how much she tried to talk herself into it.

April understood why she resisted. For one thing, she felt too old and clumsy. But no one needed to tell her that those reasons weren't good ones. There were people in the class older than herself and some were apparently even more clumsy than her. That was the point of yoga, after all. It was for everyone.

Just not ready yet, she said to herself, taking another sip of coffee and turning away from the window. Maybe she'd wait until the class moved inside and then stay way back in the corner in the dark, where no one could see her.

And that was really the problem. It wasn't the yoga class. It was that she still resisted people seeing her. Although she knew it probably wasn't true that people were judging her for her serial killer husband's behavior, she still cringed when she was out in public. It didn't matter that Ron was dead now, and that the attention of the media had moved on. Anxiety plagued her more often than she was willing to admit.

It was one reason—even though she and Seth had videoed the reconstruction of the Ruby House—she was reluctant to actually use them to promote their new design business. She was in them. What would people say when they saw her doing something so unimportant? She should be changing the world somehow to make up for her lack of awareness about her husband and what he had been doing.

To make her anxiety worse, she also felt guilty. The design business was not just for her, it was also for Seth. He had been so excited when Mimi and Janet had first given them the idea. But that was before all the secrets had been revealed. And even though Mary and Seth told her they understood, April couldn't shake the feeling of guilt. After all, when Bree told Mary that Ron was her father, their lives had been fractured, too.

But at that moment, April was experiencing even more anxiety than usual, and knew it was ridiculous. She had survived the horror of the past year, and this was just a letter. A letter from her son, Robert.

April understood that anxiety and fear were the opposite responses from what she should be feeling. After all, it was a letter from her son. That should be a good thing. Instead, she was afraid. Because it was a letter. Why a letter? What could have happened that required a letter?

When was the last time Robert wrote a letter? She couldn't remember if he ever had. The past few months, Robert texted her pictures so she would know where he was in his travels, and they had talked once or twice. Each contact was a step forward, both of them feeling their way to a relationship that had fallen apart because of Ron and his secrets.

But the relationships with both her children were getting better. Her daughter, Amanda, had been FaceTiming her once a week so she could see her grandson Noah. Amanda had promised that someday she and her husband, John, would bring Noah for a visit. "Just give us time," Amanda had said in their last call.

April knew Amanda was worried about how she would feel being in the same town where everyone knew her father. And Amanda was also apprehensive about meeting her half sister Mary and her family. April understood Amanda's fear. After all, look at how much she was avoiding things. She couldn't even get herself to a yoga class.

However, April knew that once Mary and Amanda met, all of Amanda's fears would fade away. Beside the babies, Rho and Noah were cousins and they would probably help bring the families together.

However, it wasn't Amanda who was worrying April at the moment. It was Robert. The letter looked innocent enough, but what if it was bad news?

So for a full day, April had ignored it, stuffing it into a drawer the minute she saw it. She hadn't even told Marsha about it, even though April knew Marsha would understand her fear of opening it. The letter could be something that would change her life forever, and not in a good way, and both of them had experience with that kind of news more than once just in the past year.

Good grief, get a grip, April said to herself. It could be good news! Still, she couldn't do it. She needed someone else to open it. She'd wait for Marsha to finish teaching yoga and then bring it to her to read first. Marsha wouldn't laugh or ask why, she'd just do it. And then, whatever the news was, they would laugh or cry together.

Checking the time, April saw she had thirty minutes until the class was over. Thirty minutes until she knew if it was good or bad news.

If Robert would have known the amount of anxiety he caused his mother by writing a letter, he would have just called. Instead, he took what was for him the easy way out, and wrote instead. But Robert didn't consider how long it took letters to arrive, or that his mother wouldn't open it immediately.

So neither were prepared for the result.

Eight

Cindy left the coffee shop, bubbling over with enthusiasm. She hadn't felt this good in years. *Giving up something isn't so hard after all,* she said to herself. Especially now that she had this new idea, and Judith had agreed that it was a good one.

Since she would never fulfill her dream of becoming a famous artist, she could help someone else become an artist. Or at least enjoy making art without worrying about becoming famous. Maybe that was where she had gone wrong. She tried to be famous instead of letting herself love the process of art.

She thought back to how much time and effort she had devoted to hoping that her paintings would make her a well-known painter and decided that instead of bemoaning the fact it hadn't worked, she'd think about what she had gained from the experience. After all, she had friends, a thriving business, a town that she had lived in and loved all her life. What else did she need?

Her dream would never be a reality. But it could be for someone else. If she taught art, she'd help and inspire other people. Instead of searching for fame, she'd teach how to love the process of art.

They'd talk about how art helps develop more awareness and appreciation of the world around them.

Yes, that was much more important than fame. At least, that was what Cindy told herself. So as she walked to the gallery, she planned. By the time she arrived at the gallery, she was brimming over with ideas. But first she needed to take stock of what she now had.

So, instead of going in the back door to the gallery office as she usually did, she would go in through the front door. She'd pretend that she was a visitor to the gallery. What did they see?

As she passed the large front window on the way to the door, she could see Janet arranging an end-of-summer flower arrangement. The colors echoed the colors their featured artist had used in his paintings.

Even standing outside on the sidewalk, Cindy could see how effective the lighting was in the gallery. Although they used focused lights for each picture, during the day they hardly needed them. Light streamed in from both the large front window and from the windows that used to be second-floor windows before Cindy had the ceiling removed above the gallery.

When Cindy opened the door it chimed, and Janet turned to look at the beaming Cindy. Surprised to see her coming through the front door, she said, "Boss?" Janet had started calling Cindy by that name for fun and now decided she liked it. Cindy wasn't so sure about it, but she smiled anyway. How could she help it? Janet was a picture in motion.

Although they were both about the same height—height challenged, they would often say when they called Mimi in to help with something they couldn't reach—that's where the similarities ended.

Janet's very short hair that stuck straight up, was now tipped with orange and red. She wore high-top red sneakers and skinny jeans and today she had on a long orange sweater that hung down almost to her knees over a short purple t-shirt.

Cindy thought Janet could step into the flower arrangement and disappear if she wanted to. Next to Janet, Cindy felt dowdy. Nothing she wore made her look any different from every other middle-aged woman. Perhaps a makeover was in her future.

After all, Janet and her wife Mimi had been responsible for more than one of her friend's makeovers. Perhaps now that she was starting a new chapter in her life, she could get one too.

"Got a minute?" she asked Janet. "I have an idea I want to discuss with you and Mimi."

For Janet, new ideas were like candy and caffeine combined. Checking to make sure everything was in place in the gallery, Janet followed Cindy to the back office where Mimi was finishing up with an internet order.

Mimi's long, dark hair had been arranged in an artful, messy bun on the top of her head. She had let Janet tip the ends dark red, and the light picked up the color of the hair sticking out of her bun. Mimi was a classic beauty, with an artistic flair.

Cindy couldn't help but feel a pang of envy as she compared herself to her two vibrant employees. Immersed in her pursuit of creating exceptional paintings, she had neglected her own appearance. A spark of inspiration ignited within her. Yes, it was time for a transformation—a fresh concept and a renewed sense of self. This would be the birth of a new Cindy.

Cindy motioned for the two of them to come into what they called the writer's room. They had initially set the room up for Janet's beginning writers' group. But over time, it had become a gathering room for many things. It had a tall window that faced the alley behind the gallery, so it would have always been a little dark except Seth had installed recessed dimmable lighting, making it a cozy place to meet.

Janet tucked her legs up under her on the couch, and Mimi sat in a chair at the little table where they often ate lunch. Cindy remained standing, too filled with ideas to sit down.

"Boss?" Janet asked again. Mimi cocked an eyebrow at her, not sure if it was an appropriate way to address their actual boss.

Cindy only smiled. She needed to get used to it. She knew it came from Janet's passion for watching British crime shows.

"I have an idea." She pointed up to the empty room above the office and writer's room. "Let's have art classes up there!"

It took only a second to register with Janet and Mimi what Cindy had said. Janet clapped her hands together and bounced on the couch.

"Yes!"

Mimi smiled. "What a great idea! Are you going to teach? What ages? When do you want to start? Shall we get Seth in here to start the planning?"

"Yes," Cindy answered, knowing that Mimi would take her ideas and make order out of them.

"And call April to come design it. Yes, I am going to teach. Maybe find another teacher too. Hadn't thought about ages. Maybe students older than ten and up from there. And yes, as soon as possible."

And then, looking at Janet and Mimi, she added, "And while we redo that room, I need you two to redo me."

Once again, Janet bounced on the couch, clapping her hands.

"Well, that worries me," Cindy laughed. "I need a makeover that badly?"

Janet laughed, "No, boss, I just love doing it that much."

Mimi just smiled and kept what she was thinking to herself. Yes, their boss needed it that badly. Something had been dragging her down for as long as they had known her.

Cindy put on a good front, and of course they had so many other things to contend with this year—from Bree's husband Paul's death to the discovery of Ron Page's secret life.

But now that everything in Spring Falls had calmed down, it was time for Cindy to find her own life. Maybe teaching art was going to solve the problem, whatever it was.

But Mimi worried anyway. She thought there was something Cindy wasn't telling them. Well, not telling anyone. Perhaps the art studio and a makeover would bring it out. If not, it was at least one step forward.

Mimi pulled out her phone and texted both Seth and April. They had a new design idea at the gallery. Could they come over and take a look?

Within a few minutes, both of them had texted yes. Arrangements were made. Cindy was happy. Janet was happy. Mimi wondered why she was worried.

Nine

After Cindy left, Judith lingered in the cozy ambiance of the coffee shop, savoring the warmth of her beverage and the hum of conversations around her. She let her thoughts drift to Cindy, her heart swelling with happiness at the sight of her friend's newfound enthusiasm for teaching art. Judith hoped this spark would be the key to dispelling the cloud of unhappiness that had been looming over Cindy.

She had felt Cindy's unhappiness for a while, but other things had always taken precedence. Bree's husband's death and his letter to all the Ruby sisters had brought them all back to Spring Falls. Paul's letter led to Bree finding her daughter, Mary, after giving her up at birth. Then baby Rho arrived and now Bree was a grandmother.

And it was because Paul had appointed Bruce to help the Ruby Sisters that Judith had met a man she thought she could spend her life with. She and Bruce still hadn't talked about it, but they both knew it was inevitable.

Then Nicky had come to town, bringing with her the revelation that April's husband, Ron, had been a serial killer the entire time they knew him. That discovery had almost destroyed April and her family, but they were healing. It had also brought Booker, Bree's childhood sweetheart, back into her life.

If that hadn't been enough change, a few months ago, Marsha had learned that her father, who she had never known, had always watched over her. Although Marsha only had a few days to spend with Harry Harrison, discovering who he was and his deep love for her had started the healing of Marsha's life.

Now Marsha ran a dance/theatre school in April's house with the theme, "Joy Lives Here," and everyone felt that joy when they stepped into that space. Within a very short time, it had become a favorite destination for many people. including her. Marsha's yin yoga was a weekly must for her.

Meeting her father also enabled Marsha to reveal her feelings for Nicky. Since Nicky lived a few hours away, Nicky and Marsha took turns visiting each other, exploring a new way of being.

Judith's mind wandered through the tapestry of the Ruby Sisters' shared history, noting the ebbs and flows of their experiences together. In the midst of her contemplation, a realization struck her like a bolt of lightning: Cindy was concealing something, something that was gnawing away at her heart, perhaps for years. If there was one profound lesson the Ruby Sisters had learned together, it was that buried secrets festered like invisible wounds, refusing to heal until they were brought into the light.

As this epiphany washed over her, Judith decided it was time to find out what Cindy was hiding. She was looking for a mystery to solve. This one would do, and perhaps it would lead to other mysteries to solve, other things to fix.

Casting a quick look at her phone, Judith was astonished by the amount of time she had spent immersed in her musings. Realizing she needed to head to the office for the weekly Monday morning gathering with her team of bookkeepers and accountants, she flung her purse over her shoulder and rushed out the door.

Collectively, her team played a vital role in ensuring the prosperity of most businesses in Spring Falls, safeguarding confidential information and addressing the issues that demanded resolution.

By the time Judith opened the door to her office, she was brimming with enthusiasm for the day. Nancy smiled at her boss. She had seen her as she walked past the window, talking to herself, and knew that Judith had a new project. Nancy knew that what or who that was would eventually come to light.

One thing about Spring Falls, it was a small town, but it was never boring.

Judith glanced at her calendar before the Zoom meeting. She had a full morning with multiple client meetings. Then she had a lunch date with Bree. Bree had some accounting questions to ask, and it gave them a good excuse to get together.

Later, if the weather remained this beautiful, she'd take a walk to see how the rebuilding of the police station was going. Last time she checked, the building was up, and some rooms inside were done. Enough so that Booker had moved out of the trailer he was using and into an office.

In a way, Ron had done them a favor when he blew up the station. It was old and outdated. No one had been hurt, and now they had an updated facility.

She also wanted to check on the new park they were building across the street. The owners of the house had died before Ron set fire to it, and their grown children had sold the property to the town. The only stipulation was that it had to be turned into a park in their parents' memory.

Judith had led the drive to pay for it. It would be a small green space, and since it was directly across from the police station, a very safe place for kids to play and people to sit on a bench under a tree.

Yes, Judith thought, *everything is settling in nicely, leaving lots of space for a mystery to unravel, and time to find out what was making Cindy miserable.* Yes, Cindy did a great job of hiding it, but you can't be friends with someone almost your entire life and not know when something was wrong.

That was another thing she and Bree could discuss at lunch. Maybe she knew something about Cindy that would shed some light.

Judith adjusted the blind, closing it so the sun didn't blind her clients. They were all people she knew this morning. But first, she had a meeting to run. Settling behind her desk, she switched on the small halo light on top of her computer and started the Zoom meeting.

She smiled as each of the accountants and bookkeepers that worked with her came on line, ready to solve problems, fix what needed to be fixed, and in general make sure the entire town of Spring Falls had businesses that thrived by helping each other.

Really, Judith thought, *what could be a better life than this?*

Ten

Emma decided that if she was going to grow up to be like anyone, it would be like the woman sitting beside her on the park bench. They had spent an hour talking about writing and books and birds and the changing season. Emma felt as if the heavens had opened up and dropped an angel onto the earth just for her.

At first, Emma thought the woman was just being polite. But when she asked questions, she listened for the answer. Emma knew that most people were preparing what they were going to say, or thinking of something else, when she talked.

In a bold, uncharacteristic move, Emma confided in someone else for the very first time. She expressed the emotional turmoil of constantly moving and, more recently, the unpredictability of her mother's moods. Sharing her struggles and the weight they carried felt liberating.

Bree had listened, and then told Emma that although she and Emma's dance teacher, Marsha, had never moved around that way, they both had mothers like hers. But they had found each other and a few other friends in elementary school, and that had gotten them through the worst times.

"And you're still friends?"

"Best friends. All of us. We even had a name for our little group." Pointing to the two gold necklaces she wore, each of which had a tiny red stone at the end, she said, "We call ourselves the Ruby Sisters."

Emma dropped her head and felt like crying. It sounded wonderful, but she was a loner. She'd never make friends.

"You know what makes our group special? We are all so different. I guess I am the loner of the group. Maybe you know what that's like. But it doesn't matter. The Ruby Sisters have been through some really hard times together, and come out all the better for them. Perhaps as we get to know each other better, I'll tell you all about them and what we learned."

Emma stared at the woman in front of her, afraid that what she heard couldn't be true. How could she get to know this woman who listened better?

Bree glanced at her phone. "Look at the time! It was so lovely to talk to you. I didn't notice what time it is. I should get back to my writing. But let's make a date to talk again."

"Really?"

"Really! How about coffee tomorrow at the coffee shop on Main Street? Can you be early like you were today?"

Emma nodded, trying not to smile too hard.

"I'll give you my number and you can text me if you can't make it. Otherwise, I'll see you there."

Before Bree walked away, she reached out and held Emma's hand. "Emma, it was a delight to meet you. Remember, you are a gift to life, and life has gifts for you. Are you willing for that to be true?"

Emma took her time before answering. She didn't want to be dishonest. Bree waited until Emma nodded yes, and then turned away, saying cheerly, "See you tomorrow, Emma!"

After Bree left, Emma stayed on the bench, eyes closed, listening to the murmur of the falls and the bird sounds around her. What did Bree mean by life has gifts for her? And how could she be a gift to life? She didn't think that part was true, but she was willing to believe it if it meant that she could talk to Bree again.

Then her phone vibrated in her fanny pack, and she didn't have to look to know that it was her mother. Emma knew if she listened to the message, it would either be her mother sobbing because she was worried about where Emma went, or screaming for the same reason. Neither would be reasonable.

For Emma, the saddest thing about her life was that she had lost the person who she loved the most. Her mother. Yes, her body was still there. But the woman who used to snuggle with her in bed and read her stories at night until she fell asleep, had somehow morphed into this stranger who didn't seem to like her at all.

Emma believed that the tears and anger stemmed not from genuine concern, but from a twisted sense of possession. To her mother, Emma was merely an object to be owned, not an individual with her own thoughts and feelings. The deep, personal connection they once shared had vanished, leaving Emma feeling like a stranger in her own home.

As these thoughts swirled through her mind, Emma recognized that her perspective wasn't entirely accurate. After all, her mother had arranged for her to attend dance lessons—a gesture that hinted at some level of care. Yet Emma couldn't shake the nagging suspicion that her mother's motivation was rooted in her own unfulfilled dreams of being a dancer. Perhaps the free classes were less about love for her daughter and more about vicariously living out her own aspirations through Emma.

As Emma started for home, the rhythm of her feet hitting the ground, the wind blowing through her hair, the sunlight now streaming through the clouds, her mind eased and she pretended she was running home to the mother she used to know.

Thinking of her coffee date with Bree, Emma wondered if that meant Bree could be her friend. She never had one before, at least that she could remember. And although it seemed strange that a woman that was older than her mother might be a friend, Emma decided to accept the possibility that it could happen.

And, if not a friend, at least maybe Bree could be someone that would help unravel the mystery of what happened that had turned her mother into a stranger.

Eleven

Emma had lost track of time during her talk in the woods with Bree, only realizing how long she'd been out when she saw the flurry of activity on Main Street as businesses opened their doors. She slowed to a leisurely walk, caught between the desire to delay her return home and the simple pleasure of observing the town awakening.

The growing fondness Emma felt for Spring Falls weighed heavily on her. She knew her mother could uproot them at any moment, forcing her to leave behind everything again. Despite her mother's assurances that they would stay put, Emma found it difficult to trust those promises. Still, she couldn't help but admire the town's charming atmosphere and fervently wished they could truly call it home forever.

The sidewalks of Spring Falls were immaculate, lovingly maintained by the community. An array of vibrant flowers spilled from hanging baskets that adorned the street, nestled between trees adorned with delicate white blossoms. Emma recalled her first stroll down Main Street with her mother when they had just moved to town. Her mother had shared her knowledge of the trees, identifying them as Japanese Pagoda trees, unique for their late-summer blooms.

Emma found herself continually astonished by the wealth of information her mother possessed. The innate curiosity and passion for learning that her mother had—until a few months ago—made her an exceptional homeschooling teacher. Despite the resentments that Emma currently felt towards her mother, she couldn't deny that she was well-prepared for college courses.

That day, a few months ago, as they strolled side by side, the early spring morning unfurled its promises of enchanting beauty, like a dazzling golden gem. The air was sweet with the fragrance of daffodils, and the sky was a mesmerizing azure hue so intense it was almost painful to behold.

Birdsong provided an astonishing variety of soundtracks to their walk, while the sun's warm rays bathed the street in a rosy glow. Both mother and daughter were brimming with happiness, swept up in the excitement of a new town and a fresh start.

But how could Emma have foreseen the transformation her mother would undergo, developing into someone moody and insufferable? The stark contrast between that idyllic spring day and her present reality left her baffled, unable to pinpoint what had precipitated the change.

That day, when they walked past the art gallery, they stopped to look inside at the large colorful paintings that were on display. Emma had heard her mother say under her breath, "I wonder who painted those?" and she then turned away as if it hurt to look at them.

Emma stayed a moment longer until her mother called her to hurry, but while standing there, Emma had wondered who worked there, and fancied herself inside, helping. She had wanted to go inside the gallery, and lose herself in the paintings.

But she knew she'd have to do it when her mother wasn't around, and she didn't think she was brave enough. She'd have to meet people and share who she was. That was a skill she hadn't developed and didn't think she ever would. But then, she reminded herself that she had just met Bree, and thought that perhaps she could meet people after all.

Exploring art galleries was an activity Emma and her mother often enjoyed during their travels. Though her mother didn't seem to share her enthusiasm for art, appearing uncomfortable in such spaces, they continued to visit them for Emma's sake, as the art completely captivated her.

Emma had pleaded with her mother to take art lessons, but each time her request was denied, leaving her with dance lessons instead. Emma couldn't help but feel she was living out her mother's unfulfilled dream of becoming a dancer. At times, she wondered if her own aspiration to become an artist might be her mother's worst nightmare.

It was merely an inkling, but Emma couldn't shake the suspicion. Why else would her mother's face drain of color and her hands tremble every time they entered an art gallery? Why would she opt to wait outside, or take refuge in a gallery cafe if available, rather than accompanying Emma to admire the artwork?

Her mother's refusal to buy art supplies was baffling to Emma. Most children were free to paint and draw, but not Emma—at least, as far as her mother was aware. In secret, Emma kept a box of paper and colored pencils under her bed. She also used a digital program to paint, but she longed to stand before an easel and smear real paint, watching colors drip and blend, and seeing ideas emerge from the canvas as if they had been hiding there all along.

As usual, Emma paused outside the art gallery, her eyes drinking in the display. Today, however, a woman with vibrant orange and red-tipped hair, wearing red sneakers and an orange sweater, caught her eye. The woman noticed Emma and waved at her.

Emma's initial reaction was a pang of envy—how wonderful it must be to have the freedom to express oneself like that. Her second reaction was panic. She had been seen. In a flurry of anxiety, she dashed the rest of the way home, berating herself for her hasty departure. Now, she would undoubtedly be remembered, when she could have simply waved back and continued on her way.

As Emma rounded the corner toward her house, she saw her mother waiting in the doorway, freshly groomed and dressed. Emma knew it was likely because they had to walk together to her dance class later. Her mother's expression was unreadable, a strange mix of passivity, disinterest, and anger. Not like when she was happy. Then her face would light up, and the world seemed kinder and brighter.

Emma longed for those moments and the mother she knew before—the one who laughed, smiled, and did silly things. Something had changed, and now her mother's happiness was so scarce that Emma could hardly remember the last time she had seen her smile.

As she approached the house, Emma braced herself for whatever her mother might say, opting to remain silent until prompted. Her mother, sensing her daughter's apprehension, merely stepped back inside and said, "Lesson in thirty minutes," in a neutral tone.

Emma thought that one day her mother would explode and all the things she wasn't saying would erupt. Perhaps it would be beautiful things like confetti streaming out into the air—blue, green, yellow, purple confetti floating around them like a celebration.

Or perhaps the eruption would be more violent, like an exploding volcano. Hot molten lava destroying everything in its path.

Part of Emma didn't care which one it would be if it brought back the mother she used to know. Occasional moods were one thing, but her mother was locked into them, frozen, almost like the statue on a pedestal that Emma had seen through the gallery window.

In her bedroom, Emma stashed her running gear under the bed and pocketed the slip of paper with Bree's phone number. She'd save it on her phone later, grateful for the lifeline her new friend had offered.

"Emma, I'm ready," her mother called out. Emma sighed and made her way to the small dining room table where they conducted their lessons, hoping against hope that today would be a good day, all the while knowing that life offered no guarantees.

Twelve

Marsha's class was still in session, with everyone lying on their back, eyes closed, arms and legs splayed in savasana, so when the doorbell rang, it was April who answered the door.

She had already started downstairs, letter in hand, ready to show it to Marsha, so the first thing Robert saw when his mother opened the door was his unopened letter.

She didn't know I was coming, Robert thought, and then April was crying, hugging him, and pulling him into the house.

Robert barely had time to register that they were in a fairly large room, filled with coats, purses, shoes tucked under benches before she had pulled him through another door into what looked like an office.

Holding both his shoulders, looking up into her son's brown eyes, she said, "I'm so happy you're here. Why didn't you tell me you were coming? I could have prepared so many things for you!"

And then, seeing the letter still in her hand, realized that he had.

"Oh, you did. I was afraid to open it because I thought it might be something bad."

"I'm sorry, mom. I didn't think. I only wrote it in a letter because I wanted to tell you all about the friend I was bringing with me."

"What friend?"

It was only then that Robert realized Daniel hadn't come into the house with him.

April followed Robert as he rushed to the still open front door. Still not seeing anyone, they stepped outside, where they found Daniel sitting on the iron bench beside the door, staring at something on his phone.

April glimpsed what looked like a picture of a painting on his phone before Daniel quickly swiped up to make the picture disappear. April, whose mind now automatically went to worrying if something bad might be happening, wondered what he was hiding.

"So sorry, Daniel. I thought you were right behind me."

"I figured you two needed some time together first."

"It's my fault," April laughed, holding out her hand to shake the man's hand. "I was so excited to see Robert, I noticed nothing else. I'm April, Robert's mom. Oh, of course you know that."

"Daniel. It's wonderful to meet you. It's really okay. I wouldn't mind having someone being that excited to see me. Robert is a lucky man."

As they shook hands, April glimpsed a deep sadness behind his dark blue eyes. And then the three of them had to back out of the way as members of the yoga class began streaming past with yoga mats bouncing on their backs, saying, "seeing you next time," to each other.

"Marsha's yoga class. Well, I guess that's obvious. As soon as they go, I'll show you around our little house!"

"This is not a little house, mom!"

April looked up at the freshly painted house, with its rose-colored front door, new parking lot, the beautiful maple tree in the front yard, and smiled, thinking how much she hadn't wanted this place and now how much she loved it.

"No, I suppose not. And it's much more than a house now. It's a dance-theatre studio."

Peeking around the door into the foyer, she saw that all the shoes were gone.

"Come on, I think that's the last of them. You can see the house and I can introduce you to Marsha. This is so exciting. You can meet all the Ruby Sisters. I can show you around the town!"

It was only when she said those words that April realized what had happened. Her son was here. He would meet her friends and see the new life she had built without his father. It was such an overwhelming thought that she plopped down on the bench, buried her head in her hands, and started sobbing.

"On my God, mom. What's wrong?"

"I am so happy!"

Robert looked at Daniel, silently seeking guidance on how to proceed with the unexpected situation before them. Just then, Marsha stepped outside, her eyes widening as she took in what was happening on her doorstep.

April was crying while two men she didn't know stood watching, looking bewildered.

"April?"

April looked up and pointed at Robert. "My son and his friend."

A wave of relief washed over Marsha as she realized that April's tears were those of joy, not sorrow. In that moment, she understood that April's world had been transformed once more, but this time in a direction filled with hope and the promise of a brighter future.

Watching the look on Robert's face, she saw the strong bond between them. Marsha sighed with happiness, feeling confident now that the two of them could mend what happened because of his father and move forward together as a family.

However, the friend accompanying Robert was an enigma. He stood a little apart from the others, seemingly overwhelmed by the intense emotions swirling around him. He appeared older than Robert, which made Marsha wonder about the nature of their relationship—was he a close friend or perhaps something more?

Seeing that neither April nor Robert seemed to be aware that they needed to introduce him, Daniel stepped forward and introduced himself.

Like April, Marsha saw the deep sadness in his eyes and thought, *Judith is going to have fun with this. Here is a new person in town and no one knows a thing about him. He is a mystery to be solved. Judith's favorite thing to do.*

Marsha knew exactly what to do next. They needed to have a get-together.

What Marsha didn't realize as she texted all the Ruby Sisters, asking Judith if she could organize dinner together that night, that the new man in town would completely shake up everyone's world. Each in a different way. And for one of her friends, it would feel like the end of the world.

Thirteen

The proposed Monday night gathering of the Ruby Sisters didn't happen. After learning what Marsha was planning, Robert had begged April and Marsha to put it off.

"Too much too soon," Robert had said, and Daniel had nodded in agreement.

Seeing Marsha and April's disappointed faces, Robert added he wanted to spend some alone time with his mom first. It was the perfect thing to say. April beamed with pleasure, and Marsha nodded in agreement. Robert was right. He and April needed time alone time.

So they put the gathering off for a few days until their normal meeting night. Although April was a little disappointed, because she couldn't wait to show off her son to her friends, she was also secretly glad she had him to herself for a while.

It had been months since she had last seen Robert. The last time had been right after her discovery of the truth about her husband. Robert had stopped by his sister Amanda's house in Canada where April had fled to, but had only stayed a day before saying he was leaving again.

Although hurt and disappointed, April had understood that it wasn't personal, she knew Robert was trying desperately to hide the truth about his father from himself. She understood that desire. She had wanted to run from what had happened, too.

None of them were doing well then. It felt as if Ron's betrayal had taken everything they thought their family was about and turned it all into lies. It made them all question their ability to know who people were, and that questioning gaze settled on each other first.

Now that months had passed since Ron's death, they could see more clearly that it had been only Ron who had betrayed their family. April had not. Slowly, Amanda and Robert were communicating with her. That morning, seeing her son walk in the door, April had wanted to fall onto her knees and thank whatever god brought him home to her.

As April led Daniel and Robert through the house, their eyes widened in admiration at the stunning transformation she and Marsha had achieved. They couldn't help but exclaim with delight as they took in each carefully designed space, feeling the love and dedication that April had poured into every room.

However, it was when they entered the guest bedroom that April's emotions overcame her once more. This room, which she had painstakingly prepared with the faint hope that her children might someday come to visit her, was now a tangible symbol of her dreams coming true. The soft furnishings, the warm colors, and the welcoming atmosphere were all testaments to her unwavering love and the desire to have her family close.

Tears welled up in her eyes as she stood in the doorway, suddenly overwhelmed by the reality that her long-held wish had finally come true. Witnessing the depth of his mother's emotions, Robert's heart swelled with appreciation for the woman who had never given up on him.

"Happy tears, Mom?" Robert asked. When April nodded, he added, "I love it. Thank you!"

Seeing the guest bedroom, and guessing how much his mother had worked to make it perfect for him, Robert had to hold back his own tears. He was trying to be strong for his mother, but he felt lost in the world, and he prayed that coming to this new town, and staying with his mother, he would find himself. He hoped that maybe here, in this beautiful space, he could answer the question he kept asking himself. Who did he want to be? Who was he? Was he like his father?

The clients he wrote for were growing impatient, wondering when he would go on his next journey. They craved his evocative travel articles, which effortlessly enticed readers to explore the far-off lands they were promoting. But for Robert, the once-thrilling allure of adventure had faded, leaving a hollow void in its place. Traveling now felt more like escapism than excitement, and he had grown weary of constantly being on the run.

Yet, as much as he longed for something more fulfilling, he found himself at a loss, unable to envision an alternative path for himself. The familiar call of distant horizons, once irresistible, now rang hollow and empty, leaving him yearning for a sense of belonging and purpose that had long eluded him.

"I can change anything here to make it more comfortable for you," April said. "And the sofa pulls out so you both can stay here."

They both had turned to look at Daniel, who had stayed a step behind them as they toured the house. He wanted to support Robert, but it was difficult to not let his emotions take over. What would it feel like to have a place like this that someone had prepared for him?

"That's a gracious offer, April. But if you don't mind, I need to stay on my own."

Marsha had stepped in then, saying she knew someone who rented out her small one-bedroom apartment in town on a weekly basis. He might like it. It was near the center of town and walkable to almost everything. Daniel said that was perfect. He wanted to walk everywhere if he could. He was used to New York, after all.

Marsha had made the phone call, confirmed that he could have the apartment, and drove him there. But first she took him on a tour of the town so he would know where everything was located. It was a quick tour, because she could tell Daniel was working at being polite but was exhausted. And although she had hoped he would tell her a little more about himself, he just smiled and looked out the window as she pointed out where he could eat or shop.

Since Daniel had mentioned that he lived in New York, Marsha shared she had lived in New York for a time years before and they discussed what they both loved about it. But by the time Marsha dropped him off, and they made all the arrangements for the apartment, Daniel could barely hold himself together.

As much as he had enjoyed Robert's company, and thought both April and Marsha interesting, he had missed his private time. Robert's presence had kept him from worrying about his father. And he appreciated that. But he now needed to be alone. Hopefully, he could stay alone until the group meeting in a few days.

He thought that was likely. Robert would be busy with his mom and her friends. That would leave him free to explore the town when it was quiet and no one was around. Walking helped him think, and he needed to do a lot of thinking.

The apartment was perfect for him. Small, clean, hardwood floors with dark gray throw rugs to muffle sounds. A galley kitchen with a small refrigerator, microwave, oven, and coffee pot made him smile. He peeked into the bedroom, noting the comfortable-looking bed and subdued art on the walls, but didn't go in, afraid that if he did he would fall into the bed and not get up.

Despite his protests, Marsha had taken him to a grocery store so he could get some food. Now, his stomach rumbling, Daniel was thankful for her thoughtfulness, but he wasn't ready to cook anything just yet.

So, although he couldn't wait to be alone, he took himself out to lunch. Sometimes, being alone in a crowd was the easiest place to be. Alone, but not lonely. Marsha had pointed out the coffee house and restaurants as she drove. He hadn't realized that Spring Falls had a small community college, which meant there were several interesting places to eat.

He'd go out to eat, come back, rest, and then perhaps tackle the problem of what to do with the paintings his father had left behind. Marsha had pointed out the art gallery owned by one of their friends. Perhaps he'd start there.

Fourteen

Cindy stood in the soon-to-be-artist's studio, her heart swelling with anticipation as she awaited April and Seth's arrival. She knew Mimi and Janet were more than capable of handling the gallery, and she felt a deep desire to connect with the feeling of the space before the others joined her.

Cindy's eyes glistened with unshed tears as she stood in the quiet, feeling the essence of the creative force that was waiting to express itself in this space.

She pulled the string of the one light in the room and took in what she could see of the room. It was barely habitable. Dust lingered in the air. It smelled old and musty, and she hated to think about what was hiding in the corners in the dark. A lot of effort was going to be necessary just to make it a welcoming space for artists of all ages.

First, they needed more light. She'd ask Seth to install skylights. And then perhaps put windows in the wall that would look down into the gallery. Artists could see where their work could end up and people could get glimpses of artists at work.

It might take away the mystery of creation and inspire people, Cindy thought. Although they did much of their business online, Cindy loved that the gallery was a place where people could immerse themselves in whatever art they were featuring. It didn't mean everyone had to like everything, but she wanted people's ideas about what made up art to expand.

As she waited for April and Seth, Cindy thought that during the winter it might be a good idea to display the art of crafts, from pottery to weaving. She'd have Mimi look into who they could feature. Local craftspeople first, Cindy decided.

A group text appeared on her phone from Judith, announcing that everyone should meet up that evening to welcome Robert, April's son, and his friend who had come to town.

Cindy's heart—which just a minute before had been filled with excitement about her new project, a new life not trying to be an artist but helping others explore themselves through art—closed in on itself. Within moments, all the excitement was gone, replaced with the now too familiar feeling of jealousy.

April's life was moving on. She had a son who came to visit. Was that fair? And as always, the jealousy was coupled with being angry at herself for feeling that way. April was her best friend.

Besides, if anyone needed to have something wonderful happen to them, it was April. She had lived through a year of betrayal and survived. It was only right that she find joy in life again.

Cindy wanted to be happy for her friend. She couldn't understand why she alternated between sadness, anger, and jealousy these last few months. It was totally unlike her to feel anything but joy for April and for all her friends. Instead, she had to constantly battle the bubbling up of these ugly feelings.

All because she had begun to think that life wasn't fair. Other people had love in their lives. Other people got to fulfill their dreams. Why not her?

Stop it, Cindy said to herself. *Think about the good this space will do. Think about how many good things you have in your life. Be grateful for heaven's sake.*

When that self-talk didn't work, Cindy tried something else. Using a technique Marsha had taught her, Cindy imagined putting her jealousy into a box. Then, after sealing it, imagined sending it behind her until the box containing her jealousy dissolved into nothingness.

After that, Cindy did some deep breathing, holding her breath as long as she could, imitating the videos Marsha had shown her using the Wim Hof technique. All of that helped.

And when a few minutes later she got another text from Marsha canceling the event, she felt even better knowing she didn't have to face everyone yet.

By the time she heard April and Seth's voice, Cindy felt much more like herself, and she was determined to not let those ugly feelings back in. When April breezed in happier than Cindy had seen her for a long time, that helped, too. How could she not be happy for her?

For the next hour, Seth, April, and Cindy measured and planned as they worked together to decide what to do with the room. April agreed with Cindy about the skylights and the windows and Seth said he could do it.

"It's a great idea," Seth said. "However, your gallery will be a mess for a week or more. You might think about closing it during that time. I can start this weekend. I have a small kitchen remodel to finish up. But this will be really fun to do!"

"Is that okay with you, Cindy?" April asked, thinking that if Robert stayed for a while, he would get to see her at work designing the space.

At first, the thought that they would need to close the gallery made Cindy nervous. But then she felt the flutter of excitement. Maybe during that week she could do something else. Something different. For a moment, all the ugly feelings that had been haunting her vanished completely.

But minutes after April and Seth left, Cindy sat once again on the dusty floor upstairs and cried. All the excitement she had felt while they were planning was gone, swallowed up in sadness. And she was sick of crying. Especially when there was absolutely no reason to do so.

Because despite her whiny self wanting things to be different for her, Cindy knew that not everyone got everything they wanted. She wasn't the only one in the world that had to move on. She wasn't an exception. Not everyone got to play out their dreams exactly the way they wanted them to be, and that included her.

It didn't matter that there was a time when she was sure that one day her paintings would be seen all over the world. That dream to her had been so real she felt as if she could touch it.

If she had not gone away to study, would her dream have come true? She'd never know.

When Janet called up to see if she wanted lunch, Cindy answered, "Yes please, the usual, I'll be down in a minute," and then let herself wallow for a moment longer in the past, when she had believed anything was possible for her.

Then she stood, brushed herself off, and headed downstairs, telling herself that she was looking forward to meeting April's son and celebrating his arrival in Spring Falls, and that the new artists space would be perfect, and she'd be happy with it.

Jealousy would not run her life. Cindy remembered the last time she had been jealous of all her friends' happiness—it was after they had all graduated from community college.

April and Ron had gotten married first, then Bree and Paul. Marsha went off to New York to dance and do theatre. Judith left for a few years to finish college, leaving Cindy in Spring Falls with no one.

So she had taken herself off to study with a master in New York. She didn't tell anyone. It was her gift to herself. Once she was there and settled, she thought she would surprise Marsha. Cindy had been positive she had a future as an artist, and she knew all the Ruby Sisters would be proud of her.

But that had never happened. She never told Marsha she was in town. She told no one where she went or what had happened when she was there. It had been her secret forever.

But now Cindy wondered if the fact that the jealousy and anger she felt were getting worse meant it was time to tell someone what had happened to her.

Because that summer she had lost her belief in herself, and no one had ever guessed that it had disappeared, let alone why.

Fifteen

Veronica leaned back in her chair as she watched Emma disappear into her bedroom, her back rigid with anger. Once again, they had fought over something so simple as what to have for lunch, and for the past hour, Emma had done her work without speaking.

Perhaps I should let her go to regular school, Veronica thought. *That way, she doesn't have to put up with me.* It was an idea she was entertaining, because she had grown tired of moving around trying to find adventure in life. Or avoiding doing anything important with her life.

Either way, she had decided that she was not moving again. They were going to stay in Spring Falls. It was a pleasant town, maybe the nicest place they had ever lived.

Maybe Emma would like to meet some friends. Although that didn't seem to be happening in Emma's dance classes. Marsha had taken Veronica aside and asked if she was sure Emma wanted to take dance lessons.

"Emma doesn't smile. She doesn't talk to anyone. She keeps everyone away from her by saying snide things, or turning away when they try to talk."

Veronica was grateful to Marsha for allowing Emma to take lessons on a scholarship. But how long would that last if Emma kept acting that way? Veronica knew Emma thought she made her go to dance class because she had wanted to be a dancer, and failed at it. So now she was forcing it on her daughter.

But that wasn't the reason. Yes, she had loved to dance. But that wasn't what she had wanted to be. She had chosen dance lessons for her Emma, hoping she would find that was how she wanted to express herself. Emma was a natural dancer. Why couldn't she choose that?

Veronica knew she would do everything she could to keep Emma away from art. Emma could stare through the window of the art gallery for as long as she wanted to. But that was all she was going to allow. Art had ruined her mother's life. She would not let it ruin Emma's.

"How's that working out for you?" Veronica heard in her head. It was what her foster parents snidely said to her every time she rebelled against them and attempted to choose her own life path.

Those rigid, self-righteous people had been right about that one thing. Her rebellion hadn't worked out for her. And now, trying to keep Emma out of art for her own good wasn't working either. She'd seen the box of drawing materials under Emma's bed.

Veronica sighed. It had been a long week, even though it was only midafternoon on a Monday. Sometimes she wasn't sure how she would get through the next minute. Every day felt like a week, and every week felt like eternity.

She yearned for the days when she and Emma had laughed and giggled together. When Emma thought moving around was an adventure. When all she had to think about was making sure

Emma was prepared for an unfair world while sharing the joys of life together.

Now Veronica had other things to worry about. There was Emma and her anger. And money. Something she had never worried about before. And that worry had turned her into a moody monster. She knew it. But somehow knowing it didn't seem to stop it. Veronica was terrified because, although she was preparing Emma for the world, she had never prepared herself.

Her lack of ability to be practical, to understand how things worked, to be generally a stupid person—those things people had always said about her—were true and had finally come to haunt her. And although she should have seen it coming and prepared for it, she hadn't and she didn't.

Now the money that used to arrive every month had stopped. Money that had made it possible to hide from life and only think about Emma. When she was eighteen, she had gotten a letter telling her about an account in her name, and ever since then there had been enough in the account each month to keep her off the streets.

When she had Emma at nineteen, after a fling with a boy who couldn't care less about her, the money increased a bit. Veronica had often wondered how they knew she needed more. But not wanting to look a gift horse in the mouth, she never questioned it.

But then the money stopped coming. At first, Veronica thought it was a fluke. But then she learned what had happened and knew it was gone for good and didn't know what to do with herself. She had let herself become too dependent on it and not learned anything useful about making her way in the world.

People had been right about her. Even so, Veronica knew she had to do something, anything. The rent was due, there wasn't much food in the refrigerator. She had no one who could help her.

Despair made her want to go back to bed, put a cold washcloth over her eyes, and make the world go away. But what she needed to do was find a job. As a teenager, she had worked as a waitress. Maybe she could do that now.

Not knowing what else to do, Veronica grabbed her purse, slung it over her shoulder, and then realized she had on sweatpants and hadn't brushed her hair or her teeth yet. No wonder Emma was mad at her.

Before leaving the room, Emma had hissed at her, "Get it together, mom. Find a job. Do something. Stop blaming me for your life."

Those last words had shocked Veronica to her core. Why would Emma think that? Emma was the light of her life. In a thousand years, she would not blame Emma for what happened. She knew whose fault it was. Hers. And it was up to her to fix it.

And what Emma didn't know, couldn't know, was what Emma wanted was exactly what her mother had once wanted. And knowing how it turned out for her, it was why she was afraid for her daughter.

What happened to you? Veronica asked herself. *You used to see the world as a treasure to be explored.*

But as she stood there, transfixed by her realization that she had turned into a lump of nothing, Veronica remembered the story her mother had told her. About the friend she had met that fateful summer. Both of them dreaming of being somebody.

They had become friends. Did her mother keep in touch with that woman? Did she know that her mother had a baby? And what would her mother say if she knew her daughter had done nothing with her life—the life that had held so much promise?

Is that what Emma meant? That Veronica had transferred all her and her mother's hopes and dreams to her, and since Emma's dreams weren't what Veronica wanted for her, she blamed Emma for wasting her life?

Is that what it looked like to Emma? Is that what she had done? *Enoug*h, Veronica said to herself. *Enough self-pity. We need money. I have to get it.* Twenty minutes later, changed into her nicest pants and blouse, wearing the best jacket she had, hair and teeth brushed, a hint of mascara and lipstick, Veronica stepped out into the world.

She had left a note on the table. "Went to find a job. I'll bring home something for dinner."

It was time to act like a grownup, and stop blaming life for not giving her what she wanted. She'd find work today, no matter what it took. She could do at least that much for her daughter.

Before her mother died, she had shared a note that her friend had written to her while they were in art school together. Veronica had folded it up and put it in a small beaded purse. She took it out now and read it.

"You are a treasure, my friend. Every day is a gift. Let's always look for its treasures. And in doing so, we will find life's greatest treasure, the gift of giving and receiving love."

Veronica hoped her mother's friend found that love. Her mother had been a treasure to her, and Emma was her treasure now. Perhaps she could actively try to be a treasure to someone else, too.

Veronica still wasn't sure about the perfectly loved part. But she'd do what her mother's friend had said. Take one day at a time and look for the gift it offered, and see where that took her. It wouldn't take much to be better than what she had been accepting.

Sixteen

Daniel finally decided on the restaurant that Marsha had showed him called ParaTi's. She said it was the Ruby Sister's favorite place to eat. Although Daniel knew that Robert's mother had a group of friends they called the Ruby Sisters, he couldn't remember their names. Not that it mattered. He'd meet them all in a few days, and then he'd go back to New York and figure out what to do about his father's paintings.

Months had passed, and he still couldn't bring himself to face them. Ever since his father's death, a dense fog of confusion and doubt had enveloped him, making it nearly impossible to move forward. There were simply too many unanswered questions, too many missing pieces of the puzzle.

The authorities had declared it a suicide, but that made little sense to him. His father, Cedric, had been an insufferably arrogant man, treating the world as his personal playground to bend and twist at his whim. He had always placed his own life on a pedestal, as if it held more value than anyone else's. So why would he suddenly decide to end it?

The unsolved mystery of the why hung over him like a dark cloud, casting its shadow on every aspect of his life. The paintings, once treasured tokens of his father's talent, now served as a constant reminder of the enigma surrounding his death. He knew he had to delve deeper, uncover the truth hidden beneath the surface. Only then could he make sense of what had happened, and perhaps finally find some closure.

And he had to deal with the paintings. They had been stuck away in a back room and were better than anything he had ever seen his father paint. What was his father planning to do with them? Why hadn't he sold them? Daniel hadn't realized how valuable the paintings in that room were until Steven came to look at the paintings. Paintings neither of them had seen before.

Until then, Daniel's plan had been to sell every piece of art he found. Then give away everything else his father owned. Rid himself of anything that reminded him of his father. He didn't need a keepsake to remember a man who did not know what it meant to be a father. Conquest and pleasure were his father's motives for doing anything.

A son just got in the way. A son Cedric acknowledged only because he had actually briefly married his mother. Daniel was the "official" son, which is why he was the one to inherit his father's estate, because his mother had died many years before. But Daniel had no delusions about being the only child. He was sure that at least one of his father's indiscretions had resulted in more children.

Which was another reason for selling the paintings. If he could find other children, he'd share what he got with them. He didn't imagine that his father had provided well for anyone. If anyone believed it was possible to take his wealth with him, it would have been his father.

Daniel had learned—probably by trying to be the exact opposite of his father—that he was happy with only a few possessions. And by remaining alone, he made sure he hurt no one the way his father had.

Passing the art gallery on the way to lunch, Daniel just shook his head. He couldn't deal with it yet. Besides, would April's friend really know enough about art to help him? It was worth a shot, but not right now.

He was too hungry and too exhausted to think clearly. Maybe tomorrow he'd check it out.

ParaTi's was just what Marsha had told him it would be. Quiet and charming. As he ate, he kept his head down. He didn't want to see what was going on around him, and he definitely didn't want to be noticed. At the last minute, he remembered to bring his ereader with him so he could read while he ate. As Robert knew, it was one of his favorite things to do. Read while eating.

The waitress asked him he if wanted dessert, and although he rarely did, he asked her for a recommendation. It was while drinking coffee and eating the best lemon pie he had ever had that he felt a chill on the back of his neck.

Although Daniel often tried to discount his ability to sense things, this time he was sure that it meant someone was staring at him. Finishing his pie quickly, taking a last sip of coffee, he grabbed the bill and stood, casually glancing behind him to see who it was.

Two women were a few tables behind him. He couldn't see the face of one, but the other gawked at him. Did he know her? He was sure he would remember. She reminded him of a viking goddess with red hair.

Then she smiled at him, and not knowing what to do, Daniel backed away, almost tripping on a chair behind him, and hurried to the cashier to pay.

What was that about? Daniel asked himself. *Does she know me? How? Did she always stare at strangers like that?* As he turned to leave, Daniel almost bumped into a young woman coming in the door.

"Sorry."

"It's okay. I wasn't looking where I was going, either."

For a moment, they both paused and stared at each other. It was on the tip of Daniel's tongue to say, "Do I know you?" But he knew that would sound like a pickup line, and that wasn't it at all. It just felt as if he did.

The woman's gaze took him in, her dark blue eyes staring back at him, and for a moment he thought she recognized him too. Then she smiled and turned to the hostess.

As the door closed behind him, he heard her say, "I'm here about the job opening?"

Her voice sounds familiar too, Daniel thought, and then shook his head and headed back to the small apartment he called home. He was definitely ready for a long spell of time by himself. Maybe tomorrow he'd try the art gallery.

Across the restaurant, Judith leaned over to Bree and whispered, "I bet that is Robert's friend. April said he was quite handsome, and a little shy."

"And then you scared the poor man," Bree giggled, turning to see the man Judith meant flee out the front door after bumping into a tall woman with long, dark hair.

"You're right. Quite handsome." And then, for no reason that she could think of, she said, "I bet Cindy would like him."

Judith watched the man stride past the window and then her attention turned to the woman he had bumped into.

"Isn't that Emma's mother?"

Bree swiveled in her chair to look. She was curious who the woman was that her daughter was so upset with.

"It must be. She looks so much like Emma," and then added, "She looks so sad."

Judith smiled to herself. Here was another little mystery to unravel. What was the story behind Emma and her mother? And who was that handsome man? Was it Robert's friend? And what was his story?

She couldn't wait to find out the answers, and of course she hadn't forgotten that she needed answers from Cindy, too. Judith smiled to herself. She loved solving puzzles and mysteries.

Seventeen

After lunch, Cindy, Mimi, and Janet prepared notices about the gallery's temporary closing. The construction crew had finished early with their last job and could now start early Friday morning. So on Thursday afternoon, Cindy, April, Janet, and Mimi would take all the art out of the gallery and put it in the storage room.

Because putting the windows in on the inside wall would make the most dust, Seth said they would do that part of the work first. After that, they could work while the gallery was open if Cindy was eager to open again. Seeing Cindy's face, he added, or maybe after hours? They agreed they would wait and see.

All the construction details occupied Cindy enough that the gloomy thoughts that had filled her mind lately stayed in the background. However, she knew they were there. It was like having a mouse inside the walls. Something she had experienced in her house more than once. You can't see it, but then there is a rustle of movement, or a tiny sound, and it reminds you that the mouse problem has not gone away.

It was the same with her thoughts about what had happened to her that had eroded her belief in herself as an artist. She knew when it had begun. It was the summer she went to New York to study with a master. She had saved and scrimped and her parents helped in order to afford the tuition.

The summer had started full of promise. There were four of them: two men and another woman who became her friend. The men were older, but she and Linda were just twenty, new to the world of art and loving every minute. They were determined to become masters at what they did, and they couldn't wait to share their talent with the world.

Day after day, the four of them labored in the studio under the unrelenting scrutiny of their exacting mentor. The initial weeks were a grueling test of endurance, but the thrill of honing their skills fueled their determination. They toiled for hours on end, drawing, painting, and sculpting until they pushed their bodies to the brink of collapse.

The atmosphere in the studio was sweltering and stifling, as the sun's fierce rays penetrated the industrial-grade glass, casting a harsh light on their canvases and bearing down on them mercilessly. Beads of perspiration dripped into their eyes, blurring their vision and streaking their artwork, yet they found solace in shared laughter.

They believed the mild torment would somehow elevate their craft, and by pushing through the discomfort, they would emerge as stronger, more resilient artists.

But as the weeks passed and Cindy's skills were tested, her confidence eroded. She felt her dreams crumbling like dust at her feet. Desperately she grasped at what she knew how to do, trying to reassemble her hope and belief in herself as an artist.

Each time her teacher told her that her painting wasn't good enough, she could feel the pressure building. If her work was so tragically flawed, it would lead to her failure, and her dream would dissolve into nothingness.

One day, at the height of her despair, the master invited her to have dinner with him. Just her. She had been giddy with excitement. She spent the day wondering why, hoping it was because he wanted to tell her that despite her fears, she was talented, and it was just a phase she was going through.

However, his intentions were far from what she had expected. Instead, he claimed her for his own. For a time, his increased attention and care rekindled her passion. She resumed painting with renewed enthusiasm, creating vibrant, bold works.

As she painted, she could almost taste the colors as she mixed them on the palette and then again on the canvas. She brushed and dripped, and spread layer upon layer of paint, building light and depth of color with each stroke.

It felt as if she was taking the heat of the sun and her feelings about the master and turning them into something tangible. She wanted people to feel what she felt. She wanted people to see the feelings swirling in front of them.

At first, Cindy painted her joy at being special. But then, with the growing awareness of what her teacher was doing to her, she put those feelings of despair and anger into her art and made them appear on the canvas.

Every day, he both encouraged her and made her feel worthless. Not just her. All four of them. By the middle of the summer, the two men had gone, leaving just her and Linda. Now she understood why she and Linda stayed. Back then, she thought the men were cowards, running away from a teacher who wasn't afraid to criticize while he taught.

Now she knew the men had seen through the facade of what he was doing. But that summer, she believed he treated them that way to turn them into talented artists.

Besides, he was sometimes so kind and generous to her and Linda, it would wipe out the other feelings for a time. She thought it was because they were special, more talented than the men. Even when the class was over, and she returned home, it didn't occur to her for a long time that it was only because they were vulnerable young women.

Although she had never seen Linda again, Cindy prayed Linda hadn't succumbed to his false charms as she had done. She hoped Linda was still painting, that she had thrown off any barbed remarks that had lodged themselves inside her. Remarks that had stopped her life as an artist, as if what he told her about her ability was real, that her talent was fake and completely worthless.

Perhaps Linda was wiser than she was. Even now, knowing what had started the erosion of her talent, Cindy couldn't stop the ugly growth of lies about her he had planted.

The only thing her teacher had done for her was to ensure that she would never be a teacher like him. She knew that now that she would always teach possibilities. She'd find the talent in each person, and bring it forward.

She could never live with herself if she destroyed someone the way their teacher had destroyed her. Because, for her, everything he said about her and her lack of talent became something she believed. From that summer on, she had acted as if what he said was real.

No, she'd teach art to open hearts and minds. Perhaps in the process, she could open her own heart. But if not, she'd at least have helped someone else.

Eighteen

For April, the following days passed by as though she was living in a dream—a joyful one, akin to a Disney movie. In fact, the more she pondered it, the more it felt like a Disney movie, as many of them start with a tragedy before transforming into a heartwarming tale.

She and Robert had navigated their way through the harrowing ordeal of having a serial killer as a husband and father, and were now rebuilding their lives to be filled with happiness and contentment.

It filled April with happiness that Robert loved everything that she and Marsha were putting into practice at the Ruby House, including the sign that said, "Joy Lives Here."

"It's an affirmation, isn't it?" Robert had asked Marsha and April.

"It's that, and it's an intent," Marsha had answered.

"Oh," Robert said. "A affirmation and an intent. You say it for yourself, and you intend it for others. And not just here in the Ruby House. It's what you want to do in life, too, isn't it?"

April wasn't sure if she had ever had a happier moment.

"You raised a fine young man, April," Marsha said, smiling at Robert.

Robert had looked at the two women and decided to adopt the affirmation and intent for himself. He would be a place where joy lived. He'd stop letting the revelation about his father take his excitement about the beauty and possibilities of life away from him.

For April, it felt as though the sun had burst into countless specks of light that nestled themselves within her heart. All her prayers had been answered. Robert would be okay.

Later that day, Robert and April had watched as a gaggle of teenagers arrived directly from school, laughing and giggling together as they changed clothes and headed into their dance class.

As they stood at the viewing window and watched Marsha teach the class, April pointed out the young woman who had come alone, explaining that Marsha was worried about her.

"Why?" Robert asked, watching Emma move through the class with ease. "She seems to be enjoying it."

At that moment Marsha turned and, seeing the two of them, raised her eyebrows, tilted her head towards Emma, and shrugged. April knew what she meant. Emma wasn't acting out. What was up with that?

"Well, maybe she's settled down?"

The two of them watched a while longer and then headed back upstairs. Robert said he had some reading to do, and April was meeting Seth to go over the plans for the art gallery renovation.

In class, Emma saw the looks and the shrug and knew what that meant, and didn't care. She knew they were wondering why she was acting differently. It was because she had other things on her mind.

As they moved through the barre sequence, instead of wasting her energy on resisting being what she thought her mother wanted her to be, she it let go. She had more important things to think about. Her mother could want her to be a dancer all she wanted, but today she saw a sign in the art gallery that changed everything.

They were going to offer art classes at the gallery. She was going to take them, no matter what the cost. If it was money, she'd barter. If it was her mother's resistance, she'd wear her down.

And she knew she'd have an ally. Bree had told her that morning as they had coffee together, that she understood the desire to do something so much it was like an itch.

For Bree, it was writing. If, for Emma, it was art, that was a good thing. However, Bree made Emma promise that she would stop wasting her energy on acting out, and instead direct it towards what she wanted.

Emma had promised, and in return, Bree had promised to help her with what she wanted to do. That's why Emma knew Bree would help her explain her dream to her mother. Once they met, of course.

And her mother was another reason Emma had let go of resisting being in dance class. Her mother had come home and said she had a job and then headed out later to work.

In the morning, her mother was tired as they worked through Emma's lessons, but not the tired that made Emma want to smack her mother awake. It was a good kind of tired.

"It's a nice place to work," her mother told her. "And it will bring a little money in. I'll look for more work too. And I met a woman who says she is always looking for a babysitter. Perhaps you could earn a little money too for the things that you want."

Emma had stared at her mother, wondering how one day on a job had made such a difference. But then Emma realized how meeting someone who listened to her had made a difference because it gave her hope. Maybe her mother met someone who also knew how to listen and that had helped her stop wallowing in anger and depression like she had been for the last few months.

So, instead of irritation at her mother, Emma thought she would try listening to her instead. When they were done with the lessons for the day, Emma asked her mother about her job and what she liked about it. They had sat at the tiny kitchen table with a cup of tea in front of both of them and talked.

It had been months since they had sat together that way. At first her mother had been hesitant, and then she started babbling about the job and the people there.

"Who is the woman with the baby?"

"Her name is Mary. We didn't get to talk much, but she was so kind. Her mother is a writer here in town. And her husband has a carpentry company. She was excited because he is doing some work in the art gallery owned by a friend of her mother."

As Emma listened, she wondered if there was an invisible hand at work in her life, and for once, it was working in her favor. Was it possible that Mary's mother was Bree? And Bree was a friend of the owner of the gallery?

Later, the more she thought about, the more sure she was that it was true. And that was another reason she wasn't at all worried about getting to take art classes at the gallery. Her mother was now caught up in that world, and it would be hard for her to say no now.

Moving into the second half of class, as they did combinations across the floor, for the first time Emma let herself enjoy the movement, and understood why her mother loved to dance.

Emma had discovered that when you let go, it is almost like flying.

Nineteen

Daniel spent the next few days in a kind of blissful daze. After lunch that first day, he went back to the apartment and slept for hours. Got up, made himself a sandwich, and went back to bed.

When he woke the next morning, he felt more rested than he had in years. But instead of getting up, he stayed in bed, taking in the quiet. He imagined himself drifting like a dust particle through the sunbeam that was streaming through a crack in the curtains. Then his essence would expand into the air, becoming one with the room and everything in it. It was one of his favorite kinds of meditations, one he hadn't been able to achieve since his father died.

Ever since he heard about his father's death, he had felt as if he was walking through a heavy fog. Barely able to sleep. Even when he managed a few hours, it wasn't restful. His mind kept questioning why his father had died.

Not understanding his father's death, along with his indecision about what to do with the paintings, had made it impossible to rest. And the city noise. The noise had never bothered him before, but since the moment he had stood in his father's studio and stared at those unknown paintings, it felt as if the city was pressing in on him.

Now, in this quiet town where no one knew him, he felt as if he could think. It wasn't as if he had any answers, but at least it was now quiet inside his head. Perhaps in this town, he could figure out what to do.

Following his father's death, Daniel reevaluated everything he knew about him. Cedric didn't have friends, yet he seemed to know everyone. He could be loud and aggressive or gentle and quiet, depending on what was required to remain the center of attention at any given moment.

Daniel doubted that his father ever loved anyone more than himself. Cedric always put his own desires first and could persuade anyone to do his bidding. Daniel knew his father wasn't above lying and cheating to get what he wanted. He wondered if anyone had ever truly known the man behind the facade.

It was possible that there wasn't a genuine person within the man he called his father. Perhaps Cedric's personality had completely taken over, leaving behind only a man who craved control and adoration, willing to do anything to achieve those goals.

No wonder someone killed him, Daniel thought.

And then, lying in the bed, safe from prying eyes, he let himself grieve and rage. That his father had not committed suicide but had apparently been killed was a secret he had been keeping to himself. Robert also knew, but only because the police had come to the apartment and questioned them both. Robert promised to keep it to himself. It was a news story, but only if you were part of the New York art scene where his father held court.

Yes, at first, the police had thought that Cedric had killed himself, which Daniel hadn't understood at all. His father would never take his own life. It was too valuable to him. A few days before he and Robert left New York to come to Spring Falls, the police had changed their mind. What had looked like suicide had all been staged. That made more sense to Daniel. His father had made many people angry enough to kill him.

Daniel knew that if there was an afterlife, his father was probably watching them all, smirking because he knew more than they did, and enjoying the attention. He would like it that so many people were trying to figure out who had the guts to do what probably many people had thought about doing. In fact, there were so many suspects that Daniel wondered how the police would ever find out who murdered him.

After clearing Daniel—he hadn't been in town—and then Robert, who also hadn't been in town, the investigators turned their attention towards enemies his father had. It was a long list. Daniel wasn't holding his breath that they would find the answer.

But at least it resolved one mystery for him. His father had not taken his own life. But there was more than one mystery to solve. Because the day Daniel had stood in front of the paintings in the room in the back of the studio, he had wondered when his father had painted them and why hadn't he displayed and sold them?

Stacked along the wall were beautiful, emotional, deeply moving paintings with his father's initials, C.J. in the left-hand corner. Seeing paintings like this in his father's studio, and what he had thought was his father's suicide, had made him question what he knew about his father. Now the only question was the paintings. The murder made sense. The paintings did not.

A beep on his phone brought Daniel out of his meditation. It was Steven asking when he could sell the paintings. Feeling a moment of clarity, Daniel texted back, telling him he could put all the paintings on the market except for the ones in the back room.

"But they are going to sell the best," Steven texted back.

"Don't care. Do the other ones first."

All he got in return was a thumbs-up emoji. Daniel laughed, delighted that he had decided something. And now that he had made that decision, he knew it was the right one.

The next few days, Daniel stayed in bed, made food, read books, meditated, and retreated from the world. Robert had called a few times, asking if he wanted to do anything, but Daniel had turned him down. He knew Robert would understand. No one else knew him in town. No one expected him anywhere. Steven had also left him alone. For Daniel, it was a few days of total bliss.

On the third morning, Daniel was ready to get moving again. Today was the day he would be "introduced" to the Ruby Sisters. His quiet time was over. He was rested and ready for what would come next. Or so he thought.

What Daniel could not have known was that events were coming that were out of his control. Events he would never have chosen if given the chance. Events that would make his life unrecognizable to him. And it would take him time to figure out if he liked it or not.

All Daniel would know for sure was the life he had known would never return.

Twenty

It was one of those magical, late summer, leading into autumn days that brings everyone outside to breathe the air and experience the shift of seasons. The sun was lower in the sky, changing the direction of the shadows, making everything look different.

A few red maples had begun their seasonal change of colors, altering the landscape even more. There were already a few leaves on the ground that Bree shuffled through as she walked, the scent taking her back to her childhood.

Bree thought autumn might be her favorite season. Even though autumn foreshadowed winter with his cold and gray days, that didn't change her mind. She had learned to value winter, a season of hibernation and quiet.

But autumn was glorious. Full of bright colors, sharp smells, and a burst of what she called ending energy. Get things done. Clean things up. Prepare for hibernation.

Today, Bree decided not to go to the woods for a walk, but to take a walk to the police station and remind Booker about the gathering that night, and see how the new station was progressing.

April's husband, Ron Page, had done the town a favor by blowing the station up in the spring. Yes, he had intended to hurt people when he did so, but had failed at that. Instead, it gave them a chance to rebuild something better.

Ron had been an evil man, but most of Spring Falls had turned away from focusing on what he had done, to look instead toward a better future. *April certainly has a better one,* Bree thought to herself.

For a moment, Bree's steps faltered, as she thought about what might happen when Robert met her daughter, Mary. April said Robert kept putting it off, waiting for the right moment to meet his half sister and her baby daughter, Rho. Mary hadn't been in a hurry either, saying it wasn't time yet.

Bree knew she had to trust the timing and not try to make it happen. And she knew not to predict what that meeting would be like. It wasn't easy, though. She constantly had to tell herself to stay out of it every time she tried to imagine what would happen.

As she turned the corner, Bree heard a quick bark, and knew that Addie had spotted her. But Addie, being a well-trained dog, waited until she got closer before coming over to get a hug from her.

Although never caring much about pets, Bree loved Addie. Booker had rescued Addie as a puppy. Perhaps because she wasn't pure dalmatian, someone decided not to keep her. Bree hoped she never met that person because she might want to smack them for their stupidity.

Even if she wasn't pure dalmatian, Addie had all the qualities that had made dalmatians popular as fire station dogs. She was graceful, calm, strong, and loyal.

Just like Booker, she thought as she stooped down to hug Addie, who wagged her tail so hard Bree almost tipped over.

As Booker reached down to help Bree up, he asked, "Were you out walking for words?"

"I was!" Bree answered, her heart filling up with happiness that Booker knew her that well. She had shared with him that as she walked, ideas for her books would flood in. Sometimes it felt as if the words were waiting for her and she just had to walk out to gather them. She loved that Booker remembered.

With a start, Bree realized she loved Booker. And for a moment, a flood tide of guilt overwhelmed her. How could she love Booker when Paul had been her one and only?

"Are you okay?" Booker asked, feeling Bree go rigid in his arms.

"Sure," Bree said, and turned away for a minute. She'd have to think this through, but not right at this moment.

Turning back, she smiled again, reached down to feel Addie by her side, and the world righted itself again. Paul was gone. She had a new life. One that Paul had made sure she would have before he died. It was a good thing.

"I just stopped by to remind you about the gathering tonight. And that it's at the Ruby House, not Judith's."

"Because it's not just a girls' gathering?"

"Women's gathering," Bree laughed. "And yes, that's why. All the 'boys' are coming too."

"All to meet April's son?"

"And his friend. And I think they invited Mary, Seth, and Rho, too."

"Ripping the band aid off, so to speak."

"Looks that way."

Looking around, Bree added, "The park is looking good."

"We're getting there."

Both of them stood for a moment and looked out over the space. It was only a little over a half of an acre. It was where the house had been that Ron had burned down. Bree was supposed to have died in the fire he set. Instead, she had been rescued in time.

But Ron had killed the owners days before, so they named the park after them. Friends had raised the money to turn the space into a quiet retreat. Trees were planted, and flower gardens dug. Although it wouldn't be until next spring that they would see the results, already the feeling had changed.

Booker put his arm around Bree as she shivered. He would never forget the moment he thought she was gone. Booker knew Bree was going to therapy to rid herself of that memory, but he wasn't sure he ever could. He had lost her once, and he refused to ever lose her again.

No matter how Bree wanted their relationship to be, he would be okay with it. But he would do everything he could for the rest of Bree's life to keep her safe and happy.

Addie looked up at him, and he knew she agreed. They would be by Bree's side in whatever way worked for her.

Taking a deep breath, Bree looked over at the police station across the street and asked, "Show me what's happening over there?"

Taking her hand, Booker said, "Of course." In his mind he added, "As you wish," meant exactly how it was meant in one of Bree's favorite movies, *Princess Bride*. Whatever Bree wanted, he would do his best to provide her with it.

Addie gave a quick bark. Booker knew it meant, "Me too."

Twenty-One

Today's the day, Cindy thought as she rolled out of bed, grabbed a robe, stuck her feet into the bunny slippers that Bree had bought her, and shuffled into the bathroom.

Cindy wondered how she could be both exhausted and elated at the same time. Half of her wanted to go back to bed, call in sick to the gallery, and not get well until the renovations were over, and the other half couldn't wait for it to begin.

Stuck in the past and a new start warred inside her. No wonder she was exhausted. *Snap out of it,* she said to the woman in the mirror. *Think of how many people the art studio will inspire.*

The woman in the mirror smiled, lighting up her blue eyes. Reminding herself she was helping other people always made Cindy feel better. Yes, she had more gray hairs than blond, yes there were wrinkles around her eyes, and she didn't particularly like the drooping around her jawline.

Despite that, she had everything anyone could want, and she had work to do that she loved and had wonderful friends. *Life is good,* she reminded herself as she headed downstairs to make some breakfast, studiously avoiding looking at the closed door to her studio.

Mimi and Janet were already at the gallery when Cindy arrived. Mimi was mapping out a timeline for what they would do first that afternoon to safely pack up the gallery. They planned to put all the current exhibit in the storage room that ran the full length of the gallery.

What was not visible, unless you knew it was there, was a large pocket door. It looked like part of the wall, but when it was open, it led directly into the storage room where they stored the crates and cartons the art work arrived in.

They could also access it from a regular door in the back of the office, so they could work in the storage room without anyone knowing they were inside.

Mimi had worked out an efficient system for the room. Any upcoming exhibit was stored on one end and the current exhibit packing material was stored on the other.

When each exhibit's time was over, the artwork that was sold was packed up and sent to the new owner and what hadn't sold was returned to the artist.

Cindy was proud of the fact that they always sold most of the art they displayed. It wasn't always to the locals who purchased the art. Often people come from out of town, or people purchased the art directly from their website.

Mimi was also in charge of their internet presence, and last fall Cindy had started giving her a percentage of the sales in addition to her salary. Cindy was well aware how valuable Mimi's skills were and that she could take them anywhere she wanted to, and Cindy was grateful they were being put to use for her art gallery.

Cindy had recently toyed with the idea of making both Mimi and Janet part owners. They deserved it. The gallery worked because of them. Janet was the one who made the gallery itself a destination. It was the way she presented the gallery, and how she interacted with the visitors, that often led to someone coming in to look and ending up buying.

The three of them had decided to not put the current exhibit back up after the construction was over. And while the art was off the walls, they would have the gallery painted. Seth was having his painter paint the gallery while the upstairs studio was being built.

Cindy had popped her head into the gallery, said she was there, and then headed down the street to get coffee for the three of them. It was going to be a long day, and she planned to spoil everyone as they worked.

As Cindy headed back to the gallery, carefully balancing the coffees in a cardboard carrier, she saw a girl jogging in place in front of the gallery window. Then she stopped and stared. Even from a few blocks away, Cindy could feel the attention the girl was giving the window. It was such a powerful yearning that Cindy felt tears come to her eyes.

She had felt that way too about her art. Is that what the girl was feeling? Was it the gallery that was drawing her attention? Cindy quickened her steps hoping to talk to the girl, but hearing Cindy, the girl quickly turned and ran in the other direction.

Cindy stopped and watched her. She looked familiar. But since she barely had a glimpse of her, she couldn't say why. When Cindy reached the gallery, she saw the sign in the window about the art classes and Cindy wondered if that was what had stopped the girl.

She hoped so, because that kind of riveted desire was what she wanted to help fulfill. If she could find out who the girl was, she could ask her what she most wanted to learn and start there with the classes.

Janet waved at her from inside and then held the door open for her. Handing Janet her coffee, Cindy asked, "Did you see that girl?"

Janet took a sip of her coffee before answering, "Um, yum. Excellent coffee. Yes, I've seen her a few times. She rarely sees me though, but she always looks inside like a lost puppy.

"Before you ask, no, I don't know who she is, but I have seen her walking towards the Ruby House. Maybe she takes dance class with Marsha?"

"I guess I could ask Marsha tonight. I'd like to find her and see if she wants to take art classes."

"Are we all going to the gathering?"

"Yes, April invited everyone. We'll get to meet Robert and his friend."

"And maybe find the girl," Janet added.

"Let's hope we get done in time to get there," Mimi added, taking her coffee.

As usual, Mimi knew something the rest of them hadn't expected. Maybe she knew how much work it would take to ready the gallery for the construction that would start in the morning.

Or maybe she knew it wasn't time yet for any of them to meet Robert and his friend, or find the girl. Other things had to happen first.

Twenty-Two

"It looks beautiful," Robert said with his arm around his mother. Beside him, Marsha nodded in agreement. "It does look good, doesn't it?"

The three of them were standing in the kitchen looking out over the living area, waiting for people to arrive.

They hadn't done too much to prepare for the gathering. Just added a few vases filled with sunflowers and brought in a few extra chairs. The cushions on the sofa were freshly fluffed, and they had rolled a few throw blankets up into a basket in case someone got cold. Nothing else was really necessary. The living room looked cozy and inviting, as it always did, with just the right amount of lighting and mix of furniture.

Not for the first time since he arrived, it amazed Robert to see the results of the gift his mother had for making beautiful spaces. It was a gift she always had, but now it was out in the open for everyone to see. The entire house was a showcase of her abilities, and he was proud of her. Not just for his mother's new business, but how she had moved on from the nightmare of his father.

He understood the difficulty in coming to terms with the truth about his father's actions and the person he had become, especially considering what his father had done to his mother once his secret was exposed. Overcoming the painful knowledge of his father's true nature was a struggle he faced daily.

Coming to Spring Falls had sped up the healing by helping him to see his mother differently. Not just as his mother, but someone in her own right. And she had done all of this despite what had happened. April was an amazing woman, and he was proud of her and grateful she was his mother.

Robert knew his mother was nervous about him meeting all the Ruby Sisters. But even though he was nervous about it, too, he was ready for their scrutiny. He hoped they weren't upset with him for running away after hearing about his father. A dutiful son would have stayed and helped his mother.

But Marsha had assured Robert that everyone understood. He had done what he needed to do, and besides, April always had all of them.

For the past few days, Robert had watched how his mother and Marsha supported each other and if the rest of the Ruby Sisters were the same, he was ready to meet them. At least as ready as he would ever be.

Earlier that day, Daniel had called and expressed concern about the gathering. He was anxious about meeting everyone. Besides, he wasn't family. Was Robert sure he should be there?

Robert had assured Daniel that he knew his mother's friends didn't confine family to blood relations. They were family because they chose to be, adding that he could use Daniel's support. He was meeting them all for the first time, too. Daniel had laughed and said he would be there.

Marsha had explained to Robert that Ruby Sisters weekly gatherings moved from house to house on a rotating schedule that Bree had drawn up. But this time April had requested that the gathering be at the Ruby House and everyone had agreed it was the perfect place to meet Robert.

Usually the Ruby Sisters ordered a few pizzas for their gathering and there had been some debate if they should do the same that night since Booker, Bruce, Mary, Seth, Noah, Robert, Janet, Mimi and Daniel were coming. But in the end, they decided to just order more pizzas than usual. No one wanted it to turn into something formal.

The main event would be Robert meeting his half-sister, Mary, and her family. Robert had wanted to grill his mom and Marsha about Mary before the gathering. He wanted to know if they looked like brother and sister. Did they act the same? Did they like the same things? But in the end he hadn't asked, and they hadn't said.

He was aware that he was nearly a year older than Mary. He had been born in Silver Lake, while Bree had moved away from Spring Falls before Mary's birth. Robert had learned the remarkable story of how Bree reunited with the daughter she had given up for adoption. It seemed improbable to him that Mary had eventually ended up in Spring Falls, yet that was exactly what had happened.

Marsha told Robert that many seemingly impossible things happened all the time and asked if he believed the universe worked in the favor of good. It was a question he had never considered before.

If she would have asked right after he had heard about his father, he would have said "absolutely not." But now, waiting for his mother's friends to arrive, having observed his mother's transformation, Robert had to ask himself if Marsha was right.

After all, he was getting ready to meet his sister and niece. Was this the universe working in their favor? Was the power of good in charge?

A car door slammed, and Robert walked to the window to look down into the parking lot. At 5:30, it was still light, so he could see a woman taking a baby out of a car seat. As if she felt him watching, she looked up at the window and waved.

A feeling of warmth rose inside of Robert. He could feel it burning into his cheeks and he imagined his ears were turning pink. When the baby waved too, Robert was worried he would burst into tears. He might never have met this woman, this sister of his, but he felt as if he already knew her. Was this what Marsha meant about the power of good?

Behind him, April watched Robert and knew what had happened, and whispered to herself, "Thank you, God." Marsha put her arm around April and pulled her close, and added, "Amen."

Neither of them knew that the evening was another turning point in their lives. But even if they had known the troubles that were coming, they wouldn't have changed a thing.

April and Marsha had learned that whatever trouble happened, they would face it together. Both of them believed with all their hearts that what Marsha had told Robert was true. The only true power in the universe was one of goodness, and that good always prevailed.

Cindy, working in the gallery, would have agreed with them too, but she didn't know that the next change revolved around her.

But it wouldn't happen yet. Because instead of showing up at the gathering, she texted April to let her know they couldn't come because they had too much to do to get it ready for the morning. In that way, she unknowingly delayed the inevitable. At least for a day.

Twenty-Three

Mary felt as though her heart might burst. She saw the man standing in the window and knew, without a doubt, that he was her half-brother. It wasn't merely because he was a stranger—it was because of the unique sensation that washed over her. It was as if an invisible string connected them, a bond she had never experienced before, but now that she felt it, it seemed right. Rho must have sensed it too, as she giggled and waved.

Until that moment, Mary hadn't realized how anxious she had been about meeting Robert. Would he resemble his father? Would they be able to connect? She was the product of a rape, while he was a recognized son.

Mary thought Robert might have had a harder life than her. She had never really known Ron, having been raised by the woman who adopted her and loved her unconditionally. Then, after moving to Spring Falls with her husband, she discovered that the woman she had admired from afar was her birth mother, who also loved her unconditionally.

In fact, that was all she had ever known. Unconditional love. Yes, her adopted mother, Nora, had moved them all around the country, but it had been fun. And right before Nora died, she had met Seth who helped her with all of it, and he, too, loved Mary unconditionally.

Mary knew just how fortunate she was. And now she had even more family members to love: her brother, and someday she would meet her half-sister Amanda, her husband John, and their baby Noah. If Mary could have anything she wished for, she would want them all to move to Spring Falls so their children could grow up together. *That would be perfect*, she thought. But this was perfect too—the gift of a brother. She really couldn't ask for more.

The fact that her father had been considered a monster by many felt like hearing about a stranger. She had only glimpsed Ron in town once or twice, and when she did, she felt no particular emotions towards him. Besides, she had only recently learned that he was her father. But she didn't think of him as her father—fathers didn't behave like Ron did. Fathers acted like her husband, Seth.

"Shall we go meet him?" Seth asked, reaching out for Rho, who happily transferred to her father's arms, kissing him on the check and patting his face in delight.

A daddy's girl, Mary thought, watching them.

"Go ahead," Seth said, knowing what Mary wanted to do.

Taking one last glance at Seth and Rho, Mary started running. Instead of taking the elevator, she sprinted up the stairs and straight into Robert's arms, surprising them both.

April burst into tears at the sight. And she knew if Bree had seen this meeting of brother and sister, she would cry too. Marsha, who had only recently met her father, knew what it felt like to meet family for the first time, had her camera out and recorded the whole thing.

By the time everyone else arrived, Robert and Mary were chatting away as if they had known each other all their lives. Bree had looked at the two of them sitting on the sofa, had turned away so they wouldn't see the tears in her eyes. In all of her life, she would have never imagined this scene.

Rho was sitting on Robert's knee while they talked, clapping and laughing and charming the entire room. Bree breathed a silent thank you once again to Paul, who had brought them all together with his last gift to her, and then settled beside Booker, who reached out and held her hand.

Outside, Bruce found Daniel standing in the parking lot, trying to get the courage to go up and meet everyone.

"You're Daniel, aren't you?" Bruce asked, coming up to stand beside him.

Daniel nodded.

"It looks a little daunting, doesn't it?" Bruce added, as they listened to the laughter drifting down to them, and observed the people walking past the open window.

"I remember that feeling when I met all of them. The Ruby Sisters, that is. Of course, there weren't as many people involved then. They seem to collect people. The truth is, I can never be grateful enough that they collected me, and I have a feeling that you will end up feeling the same way."

Daniel turned to look at the man beside him. "You're Bruce, right? And you belong to Judith."

"I think that's a good way to describe me," Bruce said, wondering if Daniel knew how lonely Daniel was. *Well, a dose of the Ruby Sisters will cure him of that,* Bruce thought.

"Shall we go up? I'll introduce you around. Don't worry, no one up there can hurt you."

Later, Bruce would wonder why he chose those words. Because although no one intentionally meant to hurt Daniel, it would happen. But it was not something Bruce could have foreseen or stopped even if he had known.

Besides, for the next few hours, Daniel seemed to be having a good time. He smiled, seeing how happy his friend Robert was meeting his sister.

It took him almost the whole evening before he recognized Mary as the woman waiting on tables at ParaTi's a few days before. He wondered if Mary knew the woman who he had seen applying for the job. He hadn't been able to get her off his mind.

Bruce kept his word and introduced him around the room, taking his time, telling Daniel a little anecdote about each person, so they instantly felt at ease with each other. And as Bruce had foreseen, Daniel enjoyed himself more than he thought possible. For a moment, his father, his paintings, and his death faded into the background.

"Where's the fifth Ruby Sister?" Daniel asked, after Bruce had introduced him to everyone. "I thought there were five."

"Yes, Cindy. She owns the art gallery and couldn't make it tonight because starting in the morning, they are doing construction work to make an art studio in the gallery. Mimi and Janet are there with her, making sure it gets done in time."

Because Bree called Bruce over to ask him a question, Bruce missed Daniel's reaction to what he had said.

Daniel stood rooted to the spot on the floor. It took him a moment to realize that he had been holding his breath. Letting it out slowly, he sat down in the nearest chair to think through what he had just heard.

Yes, he had known that it was a Ruby Sister who owned the art gallery. But something had shifted when Bruce said her name.

He had suddenly realized that he had come to town for this very reason. Something was wrong with the paintings he had found in the back room of his father's studio, and it was the owner of the gallery who could help him figure out what it was and then what to do with them.

Twenty-Four

The next morning, Daniel walked over to the art gallery and stared in the window. There was nothing to see. There was no art on the wall. He could see a painter's ladder and buckets of paint. Although Daniel knew that there would be construction going on, he hadn't really realized the extent of it.

It's probably not a good time to meet the owner, Daniel thought. Might as well go to the coffee shop that April told me about. Turning quickly, he bumped into a teenager standing just behind him, jogging in place.

"Sorry, didn't see you there," Daniel said, smiling at her. "Are you interested in this gallery?"

Emma stopped jogging and stared at the stranger. She wasn't supposed to be talking to strangers, but he seemed familiar, and he was staring into the art gallery the same way she stared at it.

Shrugging, thinking how could it hurt to answer, said, "Yep."

"Do you know the owner?"

"I know who she is, but I've never met her."

And then, without thinking about it, Emma added, "I'm waiting to see when those art classes start."

"Ah, an artist. My father was an artist."

"Is he famous?"

"Some people think so."

"Are you an artist?"

"Not this kind."

Emma laughed. This person was worse than her about giving out information.

"You're laughing. Why?"

"Because you are so secretive. Worse than me, I think."

Daniel smiled at the girl, surprised how comfortable he was talking to her.

"This might be weird, but if you have time, I was heading to the coffee shop. I'll buy you a coffee or hot chocolate, and you can tell me what kind of artist you are, and I'll tell you what kind of artist I am."

Emma tilted her head at the man standing in front of her. How could it hurt?

"Okay. I'll let my mother know where I am."

"Don't you have to go to school?"

"I'm home schooled and mom just started a new job, so we start later in the day now."

"Ah. Home schooled. I think I would have enjoyed that."

Seeing that the girl beside him was still jogging, and he was walking, he asked, "Shall we just run to the shop?"

Emma didn't answer, just took off. Daniel laughed and followed her. By the time they reached the cafe, they were both laughing as they walked in the door, making the few people in the coffee shop look up.

Cindy was preparing to get coffees for the entire crew at her gallery when the two of them burst in. She recognized the girl as the one that had been staring in the window. She had never seen the man before.

But when he looked around the room and saw her, for a moment she couldn't think. It was the first time in her life when she experienced time stopping. She had always thought that was a ridiculous notion. Time couldn't stop. But it did.

Then the girl whispered to the man, and the two of them headed towards her.

Stepping away from the order window, she gestured to the person behind her to go ahead, and prepared herself for what would happen next.

"Hi," the girl said. "I'm Emma. I know you are a friend of my dance teacher and that you own the art gallery. Oh, and I met this man at your gallery. He was staring in your window."

Cindy laughed. "Ah, like you?"

Emma blushed, "Yes, like me. I didn't know you saw me."

"Are you interested in art? Both of you?"

Daniel had been staring at Cindy wondering if he was losing his mind since she looked familiar to him too. Two people in one day? What was happening?

But it was more than that she looked familiar. This woman felt familiar, too. But they had never met, because if he had, he would remember the moment. Because something had happened when he saw her. He couldn't identify the sensation, wasn't sure he liked it, but it had stunned him into one of his tongue-tied moments.

Emma elbowed him and Daniel answered, "We are. But we don't know each other. We just met outside your window and thought we would talk about art together over coffee."

Then, realizing how rude that was, he added, "Would you like to join us? We could all meet each other, since we all have something in common."

Cindy smiled, "And I still don't know your name."

"Me either," Emma added.

"Sorry. This is all quite new to me. I'm Daniel."

Cindy wanted to ask what he meant by quite new. Meeting people? Or did the same thing happen to him that happened to her?

More than anything, Cindy wanted to say yes, and sit down with these two people and talk about art. Or talk about anything. But she couldn't. They needed her back at the gallery.

"I truly wish I could. It actually sounds like the perfect way to spend a morning. But the crew at the gallery is waiting for me to bring them coffee. But if you two want to meet tomorrow morning, earlier, before I am expected at the gallery, I would be delighted to take you both up on coffee and art discussions."

Emma looked at Daniel, who nodded yes.

"Great. Now you two order before me, because I have a big order."

Daniel ordered an Americano for him and a regular coffee for Emma, after asking her if her mom would be okay with that. She assured him she was old enough for coffee, and he hoped she was telling the truth.

Cindy waited behind them, wondering what was going on. *Breathe*, she told herself. *This is nothing.*

What Cindy didn't know was Daniel was telling himself the same thing. He could feel Cindy's presence behind him, and it was unnerving.

Once Emma and Daniel settled at a table near the back of the room, they both watched Cindy as she ordered and then waited for the tray of coffees. They waved at her as she left the shop. Cindy, with her hands full, nodded and smiled.

"Geez," Emma said, "Get a room."

"What?" Daniel asked.

Emma just smiled at him, realizing he hadn't a clue what had just happened. It would be fun to watch it unfold.

"So. Now that's over. Tell me what kind of art you do."

"Photography."

"Why don't you have a camera in your hand and are obsessively taking pictures?"

"I'm not that kind of photographer. Besides, I'm taking a break. Trying to think through my life a little."

When Emma said nothing, he added, "My father, that sorta famous artist, died a few months ago. It kinda threw everything up in the air for me."

Emma sighed. "I know about that. A few months ago, my mother became a stranger."

The two of them clinked coffee cups. Emma smiled at Daniel. She liked him. He would understand about what she wanted to do with her life. Daniel had grown up with an artist for a father.

It was turning out to be a good day. She had finally met Cindy face to face and tomorrow they would talk about art. Emma thought Cindy would understand her yearning, too.

Yes, things were looking up for her, and for her mom. Spring Falls was turning out to be the perfect place for all of them to be. Emma just knew that meeting Daniel would be a turning point in her life.

What she didn't know yet was if it would all be good things happening. She doubted it. Life wasn't that easy. But no matter what, she was ready. More than ready.

Bring it on, Emma said to herself.

Twenty-Five

During coffee with Emma, where they both shared their love of the arts but the barest details about their life, Daniel had learned that Bruce, the man who had introduced him around the room at the party, was an estate attorney.

It turned out that although Emma hadn't personally met most of the people who had been at the gathering at the Ruby House; she knew who they were. So after a bit of cajoling, Emma filled Daniel in with the basic details of each person's life. All he had to do was say a name, and Emma told him who they were, what they did, and how they were connected to each other.

"How do you know all that without knowing them, and why?"

"We moved around a lot. I got in the habit of sizing up people and places pretty quickly."

"Observation, a wonderful quality for an artist."

Emma smiled at him, hoping beyond hope Daniel was who he appeared to be and she could trust him.

"What's your favorite place that you have been?"

Emma sighed and then smiled. "Here."

Daniel nodded. He could see why she said that. He had only been in Spring Falls for a few days but he had already started wondering what it would be like to live there. And that was before he met that woman, Cindy, Now he felt a pull he had never felt before.

Emma didn't stay long after that. Her mother had texted and told her to get home. But Daniel remained at the coffee shop and watched the people come and go, wondering if he was serious about living in Spring Falls and what that would mean.

First things first, Daniel said to himself. After looking up Bruce's phone number, he called his office, hoping he wasn't too early. It had never occurred to Daniel that he needed his own attorney to deal with the mess his father left him.

Bruce had answered his own phone, and said he was free right at that moment, so why not come over now? His office was only a few blocks away from the coffee shop. Daniel took that as a sign that he was doing the right thing and told Bruce he'd be right over.

In the future, Daniel would think of that Friday morning as the moment he made an actual decision to turn his life around. It started with bumping into Emma, then standing star struck in front of Cindy, and then asking Bruce for help. Actually asking anyone for help. But it was Bruce that started the ball rolling that would steamroll over what he had known, and reveal what his life could be.

Bruce welcomed him into his home office and then asked if he was more comfortable sitting in the official office or would he like something more informal. Daniel chose informal, and they ended up in Bruce's kitchen where he made a quick breakfast of scrambled eggs and toast, which they ate sitting on bar stools around the kitchen island.

Bruce filled Daniel in on how he had gotten to Spring Falls. It started with his friend Paul's last letter to his wife's friends. Then how he had met Judith over the phone and realized the life as he knew it was over. A few months later, he sold his practice and moved to Spring Falls.

"Do you ever regret it?"

"Not for a moment. It was the best decision I ever made."

Bruce gave Daniel time to think about what he had said, and then asked, "Are you in that kind of pivot moment, too?"

"I think I am."

"Do you want to tell me about it?"

When Daniel nodded yes, Bruce asked, "As an attorney or friend?"

Daniel laughed. "Can I have both?"

"You can. I am delighted and honored to be both."

After discussing what being his attorney would mean, and Daniel had signed their business contract, Bruce took out his tablet and said, "Tell me the story."

At first, Daniel hesitated, not entirely sure he could tell anyone the entire story, but once he got started, he couldn't stop. As Bruce listened, taking notes as needed, Daniel felt hopeful for the first time in years. Maybe ever. And that was news to him. He hadn't realized how burdened he was by who his father was.

"So, you are the only officially recognized child of your father's?"

"Yes, because he actually married my mother. They divorced not long after, once my mother realized what kind of man he was, but they stayed in touch. I saw him a few times a year. I think he hoped I would be more like him. I know I was a disappointment to him."

"But he specifically made you the beneficiary of his estate. No one else?"

"Weird isn't it? But perhaps he hoped I would carry on his legacy since I have his name. Although I use my mother's maiden name for my photography work, I never changed my official name."

"To be clear, besides setting up your own estate plan, you want me to help find any other siblings you might have because you want to share your father's estate with them? Many people would ask 'why bother'?"

"It's partly because I want to share his legacy. Not the way my father thought I would, but by sharing his wealth. And it's also because I would like to have more family.

"My mother passed away when I was a teenager, and I have been mostly on my own since them. Perhaps that is partially why this town and your friends are so intriguing. You all have each other. You've made your own family."

Bruce smiled, "We have. Like you, I came here without family, and now I have all these friends. Perhaps if you don't find any siblings, you will stay and find a family here."

"Perhaps," Daniel said.

"We might need more help to find your siblings. How do you feel about asking Judith for help? She loves solving mysteries. And if anyone can organize a search for them, it would be her."

Thinking of the red-haired woman he had met the night before, Daniel thought she would be a wonder to see in action.

"Sounds good to me."

"Her secretary and mine are the same person. Nancy will know if Judith is free."

As Bruce made the phone call, Daniel checked in with himself. Was he doing the right thing? Although he was honest when he said he wanted to find out if he had any siblings, he was afraid, too.

After Bruce hung up saying Judith was available now, Daniel said, "I omitted one very important part. It's something that might change everything. I told you my father died. But it's more than that. At first they thought it was a suicide, then they discovered he was murdered. What if it was one of his children?"

"You kinda buried the lead here, Daniel. You met Booker last night too, didn't you? Perhaps he should be at the meeting too?"

Numbly, Daniel nodded. This is why he had kept this all to himself. Now it was too late. For better of worse, he had started the ball rolling and now there was nothing he could do to stop it.

Twenty-Six

Cindy walked back to the gallery, balancing the coffees on their cardboard tray, wondering if she had imagined it all. and decided that she had. Besides, once she walked into the gallery and saw what was happening, all thoughts of what she felt when she met Daniel flew out of her head.

The gallery was alive with the sound of hammers and drills. The entire floor was sprinkled with dust and shards of plaster, and looking up, she could see the workmen cutting through the walls to make the windows into the studio space. As she stepped inside, the noise grew louder, and the air was thick with the scent of sawdust and sweat.

It's a marvel, Cindy thought, *that all this dust was a wall just the day before.*

The light from the front windows made the airy space glow with a pale, golden hue as the sunlight hit the dust in the air. Cindy stood inside the door with her mouth open. She had forgotten what a mess this would be. She had lived through it before when they had built the gallery. She knew it would get better. But in the meantime, it was a disaster.

The last time she had been in this situation was years before, when she first opened the gallery. Back then, she had only been leasing the space. Now, with Judith's help, she owned the building. This time, she wasn't starting a business from scratch. She was expanding it.

Back then, she had eagerly anticipated the day she could open the doors and have the gallery full of people admiring her art. Eventually, the dust had cleared. She had covered the walls with beautiful art, and the gallery opened for business. However, she had never hung a single piece of her art.

That's enough of that kind of thinking, she told herself.

"Coffee!" Cindy called out, and all the noise stopped. Cindy took the coffees into the Writer's Room thinking she should have brought food too. At that moment, Judith walked in the back door with a tray of cinnamon buns.

"I thought you all might like a celebratory treat!" Judith said.

"Wow," Seth said, "Thank you!"

The two men working with him smiled and mumbled thank you, their mouths full. They had heard rumors about how good Judith's cinnamon buns were, and after one bite decided the rumors were true.

As they ate, Seth shared his plans for the day with the women. He hoped to have all the windows in and sealed so they could clean up the gallery space, and his painter could get that done while they worked in the studio space. First the skylights, then they could move on to the walls and floors.

"It's going to be beautiful, Cindy," Seth said. "And soon as little Rho is old enough, she is signing up for art lessons here and dance lessons at the Ruby House."

"Like Emma," Cindy said, and then realized not everyone knew who she meant, so added, "I just met her at the coffee shop. She takes dance classes from Marsha."

Once the men had returned to the room upstairs, and Mimi and Janet had returned to the office, Judith turned to Cindy.

"What's different about you? Did something happen?"

"Of course it did. The whole gallery is a mess. Everything is different."

"No, I don't mean that. I mean you. Did something happen?"

Cindy sighed, thinking about the encounter that morning with Daniel. That had to be what Judith was referring to.

"Judith, are you a witch or something?"

"So what is it?"

"Nothing really. I went to get the coffees, and that's where I saw Emma. She was having coffee with some guy named Daniel."

"Daniel? Robert's friend?"

"You know him?"

"Sure, he was at the gathering last night. Bruce found him outside, staring at the building. Bruce said he thought he was trying to work up enough courage to go in, so he took him under his wing and introduced him around."

"What else happened? I'm sorry I missed it."

For the next few minutes, Judith filled Cindy in with who had been there and how much fun it had been. She shared that the best part happened when Robert and Mary met, and how happy it made April and Bree.

"But, enough of that. Nice diversion tactic Cindy, what about Daniel?"

Cindy blushed and shook her head. "Don't really know. It was just weird. And besides, I keep thinking, I know him. But how? What's his full name?"

Judith held up a finger as she answered her phone.

"That was Nancy. Bruce is bringing Daniel over to the office. Not entirely sure why, but I'll fill you in on what I learn, because I actually don't know his last name. All I know is he is a photographer and has lived in New York most of his life."

After Judith left, Cindy took a moment to gather her thoughts. New York. She had gone there just a few months ago. She had visited several art galleries while she was there. Perhaps she had seen him at one of them?

As Cindy cleaned up the coffee cups and covered the buns so the workers could have more later, she tried to remember where she had met Daniel before and then decided that she was mistaken. She would have remembered him if she had.

Twenty-Seven

"I heard you met Cindy. How is she doing?" Judith asked Daniel as soon as they were all seated.

Daniel had just taken a sip of coffee, and for a moment he struggled to swallow. "She's doing well," Daniel said, a bit too quickly. "I mean, she is doing fine. Actually, I have no idea. I just met her for a moment."

Judith smiled to herself. She was right. There was something happening between the two of them. Cindy's blush and silence had given her away, and now Daniel was stuttering.

She remembered how much she had resisted the feelings she had for Bruce and wondered how long the two of them would resist each other. She thought perhaps she could speed up the process for them, but first she had to make sure that Daniel was what the Ruby Sisters called a "good guy."

It was perfect that he was sitting in her office, getting ready to tell her his story.

"She seems really nice," Daniel added after collecting his thoughts and putting his coffee down on the side table that sat between his and Bruce's chair.

Nice? He said to himself. *That's how you describe her? Get a grip.*

Taking a deep breath, he calmed himself down, and tried not to think about how he was making a fool of himself. He squinted at Judith because she had the blind open in the window behind her, making it hard to see her, and wondered if that was on purpose.

Later, after he told her more about his story, Judith stood and closed the blind and switched on soft overhead lights so he could see her perfectly. He realized he had passed some kind of test. He wasn't sure if he had passed her business test or a Ruby Sister test, or both. He hoped it was both.

Despite initially convincing himself that the familiarity he felt when he met Cindy was a mere coincidence, Daniel couldn't help but question if he was deceiving himself. Not only did she feel familiar, but Cindy also looked familiar. How that could be remained a mystery.

Daniel dragged his thoughts back to the room and waited for Judith's next question. Telling the story was taking longer with Judith than it did with Bruce. Daniel realized that was another reason Bruce brought him there. With Judith, he would share details he might forget to tell Bruce. It was a good double teaming.

Daniel was grateful that Booker couldn't be there though, because having Judith question him was enough. She was gentle, but meticulous, and relentless. But as uncomfortable as Daniel was with the questioning, he was also grateful. He wasn't carrying this burden by himself any longer. Having finally decided to get help, he knew it was the right time and the right people.

On the way to Judith's, Bruce told Daniel that Booker was out of town visiting Nicky and her sister Sara. When Bruce remembered Daniel didn't know who he was talking about, he explained Nicky was the woman who had brought to light the truth about Ron Page, and her sister, Sara, was Ron's first victim.

Booker often went to Jakestown unofficially. This time, Marsha had gone with him. Booker always said he went there to eat at the diner, but really he was checking in on the sisters. Yes, Ron was gone, but Booker wanted to make sure the two women were still on track to rebuilding their lives. And because Marsha and Nicky had started seeing each other a few months before, it made sense for her to tag along.

Booker's office said he would be back that afternoon, so he and Bruce made an appointment to see him later. It would only be a formality. Neither of them thought that there was anything Booker could do to solve a murder case that happened in New York, but Daniel wanted Booker to know about it just in case.

After asking questions for almost an hour, Judith said she had enough for now. She would start a search for any siblings Daniel might have, using her computer guy, Matt. Judith also took three DNA swabs from Daniel, while sharing that was how Mary and Bree had found each other. She'd send them to CRI Genetics, Ancestry, and 23andMe and see what they came up with.

She also arranged to have all of Daniel's father's business records sent to her. Judith said, "We'll follow the money," and then laughed. "I know that sounds cliche, but that's where the answers to what people do are often found. Have you looked through them?"

Daniel shook his head. "I wouldn't know what to look for. I barely understand my own accounting."

She said that Booker might also be willing to run a search, especially since there was some mystery surrounding his father's death.

As Daniel stood to go, Judith suggested he talk to Cindy about his father's paintings. Or if he wasn't ready to talk about them yet, just get to know her better. She might have contacts in the art world that could help him.

Daniel smiled as he answered, "Emma and I are having coffee with her in the morning."

"Perfect," Judith said, and meant it.

The meeting with Booker didn't last long, for which Daniel was grateful. He wasn't sure if he had ever been so exhausted. He couldn't remember the last time he had talked to so many people in one day.

I*t was only five people*, he said to himself. But to him, that was a crowd. He was used to spending days and sometimes weeks on his own. Daniel knew himself well enough to know if he lived in a place like Spring Falls, he would have to learn to pace himself.

But the day had been a good one. He had asked for help from people that could help him. He was no longer the only one looking into his father's life. Besides, he hadn't really done anything other than think about it and hold off Steven, who wanted to sell all the paintings.

Daniel wasn't sure why he clung to those last paintings. The simplest course of action would be to sell them and set aside the money until they could determine if any siblings existed. His father rarely made mistakes, so it was possible that he was the only child. However, his father was also a fool. And Daniel had a strong feeling that there might be at least one more person deserving something from his father's estate.

As Daniel settled into bed with a book, even earlier than normal, knowing he needed a good night's sleep before his coffee meeting with Emma and Cindy, he thought that if anyone could find out the truth, it would be Judith.

And as much as he thought he was ready to discover it, Daniel also knew finding out the truth about his father frightened him. Would he be able to deal with what she found?

Too late now, he thought to himself as he drifted off to a restless sleep, his head filled with unanswered questions.

Twenty-Eight

Emma came home after having coffee with Daniel and found her mother sitting at the kitchen table, waiting for her. The house smelled like eggs. Had her mother made her breakfast? If so, the eggs weren't there anymore. Did she throw them away? Was she mad at her?

Even if she was mad, it was better than coming home and finding her lying in bed with a cold pack on her eyes, trying to disappear from the world. As if the world was like peek-a-boo. Emma had figured that game out long ago. Just because you didn't see the world didn't mean the world didn't see you.

"Where were you?"

"Running."

Veronica sighed. She supposed she couldn't ask her daughter to stop running. But it was hard not to worry knowing Emma was out there on her own.

Before her mother could ask her more questions, Emma asked her how work had been, and then kept prompting her to keep talking. So by the time her mom had described the night at the restaurant, it was time to get down to the morning's school work.

Not that Emma didn't want to tell her mother about the morning. In fact, she was itching to share. She had met three people who could help her with her desire to be an artist. But they were all strangers, so what would her mother say about her talking to them?

As the morning wore on, Emma kept thinking about Daniel and Cindy, and Bree from the day before and finally when her mom asked her what she was thinking about, since she seemed so distracted, Emma gave in and told her about coffee with Daniel and meeting Cindy. She didn't tell her about meeting Bree at the falls, saving that for another day.

And Veronica reacted just the way Emma thought she would. Angry, upset, worried. "What were you thinking, having coffee with a strange man?"

"I was thinking he wasn't strange. It was in a public place, and everyone in the coffee shop knew Cindy when she came in. So it was perfectly safe. Besides, I want to take classes at the Cindy's art gallery once the studio opens.

"Come on, mom, I know you know what it feels like wanting to do something so much that it's on your mind all the time. You used to dance. Didn't you love it?"

Veronica sighed, thinking how much she had been dreading this day, putting it off forever. But it was time to tell the truth.

"I did love to dance. But that wasn't what I thought about all the time. I wanted to be like your grandmother."

Emma sucked in her breath. She had seen pictures of her grandmother, but she had died long before she was born. She knew that she and her mother looked like her grandmother. They were all tall, had dark blue eyes and dark hair. But that's about all she knew about her.

Emma didn't even know her grandmother's real name. When she was younger, she'd asked her mother all the time about the past and then gave up when her mother wouldn't answer her. Was she ready to tell her now?

Veronica sat still for a moment, realizing that she had just told Emma her biggest secret and the world hadn't fallen in. In fact, now, in this moment, with the sun shining through the cracks in the blinds, revealing how dingy and dirty their apartment was, she realized that the time had come to tell Emma all of it.

Emma was old enough to understand. She'd probably been old enough all along. She was the one who hadn't grown up enough to take responsibility for her life, and she had dragged Emma down with her.

Well, she hadn't dragged Emma down at all, because Emma had always stood up for herself, and now she realized how grateful she was that Emma had resisted all her attempts to change the trajectory of her life.

"Thank God you are who you are, Emma," Veronica said. "You haven't let me or life drag you down."

"You're scaring me, mom. What are you talking about?"

Veronica looked around at their crappy living room and realized she didn't want to tell Emma about her life in such an ugly place. Her daughter knew the town better than she did. Perhaps she knew some place beautiful and peaceful.

"Do you know someplace we can go to talk? Someplace pretty and private?"

"We could go to the falls. There's a nice trail to it, and a few benches to sit on."

"Show me."

They drove in silence, Emma having put the address into her mother's phone. They parked and walked the trail without speaking. Both of them were engrossed in their own thoughts, saving what needed to be said until it was the perfect place to say it.

Emma thought how different it was to walk the trail instead of running it. She saw so much more. Small wind gusts sent leaves twirling down on them, and she could imagine them as letters from the fairies that lived in the forest.

Not that she truly believed that there were fairies, but then why not? Imagination had fueled her childhood. Why should that stop her now?

Emma pointed to one bench that sat in dappled shade. Her mom brushed it off with a piece of tissue she had in her purse and sat down. Taking a deep breath, she reached into her purse and pulled out a photo and a small beaded purse which contained a deeply folded piece of paper.

She handed the photo to Emma. "This is your grandmother when she was in New York studying to be an artist."

It only took a moment for Emma to recognize her grandmother. There were only two women in the photo. One tall and dark, one short and blond. And two men. It was obviously an art studio. Canvas sat on easels in the background and brushes in jars sat on the table.

"Who are the other people?"

"I don't know. I just know this was taken in an art studio in New York. She was just twenty then."

"Did she ever become an artist?"

"She never had a chance. She got pregnant with me that summer, and that dream was over for her. Then she died when I was a little older than you. Until then, I dreamed of being an artist too, like my mom. And now like you. But she died, and that ended that."

"You had foster parents," Emma said. She knew that much.

"Yes, terrible people, really. No imagination. No desire to have an independent child living in their home. They discouraged everything I did. Told me I was useless. There was no art allowed. I didn't want to anymore, anyway.

"As soon as I turned eighteen, I left. And then, not long after, I did the same thing as your grandmother. I got pregnant. But I was glad because now I had someone to love.

"My mother always told me I was her treasure. That she didn't mind not being an artist. Instead, she taught me about the treasures of the world.

"I understand what she meant about treasures. You were, are, my treasure. I wouldn't trade you, or my life, for anything.

"But I want you to experience more about life. I wanted you to be anything you want to be. Except an artist. Now, I realize I was wrong. But I hope you can understand why. I thought that art destroyed my mother's life, and I didn't want it to destroy yours."

Seeing the piece of paper in her mom's hand, Emma asked, "What's that?"

"Mom gave this to me when I was your age. This is the note she received from her friend at art school that summer. I thought I would give it to you now. And then perhaps we can look for the treasures of the world together.

Unfolding the note, Emma read, "You are a treasure, my friend. Every day is a gift. Let's always look for its treasures. And in doing so, we will find life's greatest treasure, the gift of giving and receiving love."

Emma looked up at her mother and smiled through her tears. This was the mother she missed, and now she was back.

"Yes, mom, let's find treasures and do it for grandma."

Twenty-Nine

Emma barely slept that night. She was happier than she ever thought was possible. Everything was different. Or at least it was on the way to being different. After their talk in the woods, she and her mother had stopped at the craft store just outside of town, and her mom had bought her an easel and a few art supplies.

It wasn't much. Her mom had said they didn't have enough money to buy more, but now that she was working, she'd keep a little aside for Emma and her art.

Emma could see how worried her mother was about money, but let that conversation slide. She'd deal with what had happened that made her mother worried about money later. In the meantime, she'd start doing something, maybe babysitting Bree's granddaughter to bring in her own money for art supplies and maybe new clothes.

Still, now her art supplies were out in the open, which felt like the greatest gift ever. And a new canvas was sitting on a new easel waiting for her. No more hiding. Now that she knew her grandmother had been an artist, she could start looking for more information about her. Maybe even find out where that art class had been.

First, I need to find out her full name, Emma said to herself. For some reason, her mother had not told her and she had forgotten to ask. Was that on purpose? And she didn't know a thing about her grandfather, or even her father. What was up with that? What was the big secret?

All she knew was her father was a one-night stand, and that he never even knew her mother was pregnant. Where did that happen? Was he older? Would he have wanted her if he had known about her?

Emma doubted it. Otherwise, why wouldn't her mother have told him? Maybe because they were much too young to be having kids? At least she knew her mother was.

That is not something I plan to do, Emma thought. *No kids, at least not for a long, long time. I have no desire to be like my grandmother and mother in that respect.*

As Emma lay awake, trying to puzzle out the mystery, she thought about the problem with their money. They always had some from somewhere. Why? Where had it come from all those years, and why did it stop?

Emma realized that now that she had a little information, she wanted more. Questions filled her head. What were the names of her relatives? Where were they?

She told herself to stop asking. She had to let it go for a few days. Give her mother time to process what they had done so far. The only decision she had to make was if she was going to go running before she met up with Daniel and Cindy at the coffee shop in the morning.

Her mom was sound asleep, having worked late into the night at ParaTi's. Emma had heard her come in, open the refrigerator, probably to get water from the pitcher they kept in there, and then peek in her door to check on her.

Emma had pretended to be asleep, but she heard her mother whisper, "I love you," as she closed the door again and headed to her room.

Emma had whispered back, "I love you, too," once she knew her mother was where she couldn't hear her. This was a habit she was going to have to break—hiding her feelings—but at the moment, it was the best she could do.

After hours of being awake, Emma eventually fell asleep. When she woke in the morning, she decided she wouldn't run first. She was too tired and went back to sleep.

She woke up an hour later, realized she had only fifteen minutes before she was supposed to be at the coffee shop, jumped out of bed, threw on the clothes she had laid out the night before, brushed her hair and ran out the door. She had told her mother where she was going, so there was no need to leave a note.

Daniel and Cindy were standing in line, waiting for coffee, when she burst through the door. They both turned to smile at her, and she smiled back, thinking this was the best day ever. Once again, she wondered if the two of them already knew each other somehow. It was if they were already connected with an invisible cord.

Maybe lots of people are connected that way, Emma thought. But then they were asking her what she wanted, and she forgot to look around the coffee shop to check out her theory.

Minutes later, they were at a table and all their attention was on her. And then, to make her day even better, Bree walked in the door, waved at the three of them, and then stood in line to order.

"I was talking to Bree yesterday after we met, and she said she knew you, and asked if she could join us," Cindy said.

Emma's eyes filled with tears. All three of them were there for her? How could that be? It was like that note her mother showed her. If she looked for treasures, she would find them?

For the next hour, the four of them talked about everything that was important to Emma. Art, life, what they were doing, what she was doing. Cindy assured Emma that she could come to any art class she wanted to attend. They'd work out some kind of trade. And Bree said she was sure Mary would want her to babysit. After all, Mary and her mother knew each other now. They both worked at ParaTi's.

This was another piece of news that made Emma wonder why she had never noticed how interconnected life was. Or was it just in Spring Falls? That couldn't be true. It was just something she had not thought about before. And as they talked, Emma started envisioning making art that would somehow depict that awareness.

"I'm heading over to Mary's right now," Bree said to Emma as she got up to leave. "Would you like to come with me?"

Emma was pretty sure she might burst out giggling. She was so happy. But she managed to just say, "Yes, please."

Watching the two of them leave together, Cindy asked Daniel if Emma felt familiar to him. He nodded and then said, "But then, you do too."

Cindy nodded, knowing what he meant, and then asked, "What are you doing later today?"

"Are you asking me out?"

"Kinda. I have to check in with the construction at the gallery, but then perhaps lunch and then I can show you around town?"

"Can't think of anything I would rather do," Daniel answered. "And perhaps in the process we can tell each other more about our lives, and figure out if we have met before. Or if it was another lifetime."

Cindy laughed. "Oh. You believe in that, do you?"

Daniel smiled and said, "Why not?"

"Yes. Why not?" Cindy answered, thinking of the time the Ruby Sisters had watched Bree's husband leave this one life and head to another. What did they know about things like that? Maybe that was why Daniel felt so perfect to her. They already knew each other from another lifetime.

But I don't have time to fall for someone, Cindy thought. Especially someone that she knew nothing about. Still, she used to expect to find treasures in life. Perhaps Daniel was a treasure, one that came to her, and she should accept it.

We'll see, she said to herself. But that was something she had believed long ago, and now she wasn't so sure that it was true.

Thirty

Sunday morning, Daniel woke up to a text from Judith that included the Ruby Sisters and the men in their lives. He stared at his phone, wondering how that happened.

One afternoon with Cindy, and now he was part of their circle? How was that possible? And did he mind?

Are you crazy? Daniel asked himself. *Why would you mind? This is a good thing.*

Daniel realized he must have passed some kind of test for him to be included so quickly. But that inclusion scared him for more reasons that he could put into words. Instinctively, he knew it meant he would be required to share. Not just everyday things. Bigger things. Things about his father. Things about his life.

You are a stone cold idiot, he said to himself. So what? Isn't it time? Besides, he had already started sharing secrets. Judith, Bruce, and even Booker knew some of them.

But not Cindy. And Daniel knew that was who he was worrying about.

They had spent a wonderful afternoon together. Cindy took him for a walk in the woods where autumn was just beginning.

He often walked in Central Park, but the woods were different. No people. Wilder. Full of birds, colors, smells of leaves and late summer flowers.

They ended up on a bench by the falls and sat quietly together. Daniel wasn't sure he had ever felt so peaceful.

"You look happy," she said, and Daniel had smiled and said that he was. They both left it at that. Daniel wondered how one person, who he had just met, could make him feel so different.

After eating lunch at ParaTi's, they had sat in the new park across the street from the police station. Cindy had told him the story about the park and the house that had burned down.

He had listened in horror as Cindy told him how Ron had planned to kill Bree and as many other Ruby Sisters as he could just to get April back. Hearing the story, Daniel wondered how much of it Robert knew. And if he did, how guilty would he feel for not being there for his mother right after it had happened? It had taken Robert months to visit his mother.

But Daniel knew Robert had done what he needed to do to work through the knowledge that he had a serial killer for a father. And after meeting April, Daniel thought she probably understood that, too. And, seeing how the Ruby Sisters worked, Daniel knew that no matter what Robert had done or not done, what counted to all the Ruby Sisters was that he was here now.

And so am I, Daniel thought, staring at the text.

"Sunday brunch at ParaTi's?" the text read. As his phone started dinging, he realized already everyone was answering yes, except him. Thinking he was an idiot for stalling, he answered yes, too.

As he headed to the shower, Daniel let his thoughts drift back to his day with Cindy. Everything about it had been perfect. But when he had asked her why she didn't show her art in her own art gallery, he had felt the shift in her. It was as if a door had closed and she was thinking about not answering him.

But then, relaxing a little, Cindy told him ever since she was little she thought she was an artist. She had actually believed, falsely it turned out, that she would be famous one day. But in her early twenties, a master teacher had told her she had no talent, and somehow what he said had changed her ability to paint.

"You believed it as if was real," Daniel had said to her. "What if he didn't know what he was talking about? Remember what John Lennon said, 'Every child is an artist until he's told he's not an artist.'"

Cindy looked up at him, her blue eyes catching a ray of sunshine, and for a moment didn't speak. Then she shook her head. "No, he was right. I should have accepted it years ago." And then she changed the subject, and he didn't press her for more information.

He had let it go. It was her private life. She didn't need to share everything. After all, despite the feeling they had met before, they had only spent a few hours together. And if he stayed in Spring Falls, they would have plenty of time to share. Perhaps she would show him her art, and he could encourage her, because he knew that whomever that teacher had been, he had been wrong.

As Daniel dressed to go out, he realized it was just a week ago that he and Robert had been in New York, and Robert had asked him to come to Spring Falls with him, and he had said yes instead of the no that would have been his normal response. Pulling a soft blue t-shirt over his head, Daniel asked himself, how could so much be so different in only seven days?

But then, sometimes things change in a flash, Daniel thought, remembering the phone call he had received telling him his father had died. Not that he grieved his father. How could he? His father was distant and cruel. All his life, he had reminded himself that the things his father said about him weren't true.

So, truthfully, he was glad his father was dead. No more evil words would escape his mouth to hurt him or anyone else. But that phone call had changed everything about his life. He had been living a private contemplative existence, where he did his best to avoid all subjects that involved his father, and now it was to one where he had to take care of his father's legacy.

Privacy and silence were two of the reasons he loved photography. As a photographer, he was an observer. He didn't have to speak. He recorded what he saw so others could see it, too. Photography could reveal the true essence of something.

Sometimes, instead of taking digital photos, he used film and then processed the film himself. He loved seeing the image revealing itself, slowly coming out of the ether into reality.

That's what his life felt like at the moment. A picture was being developed. All that had been hidden was revealing itself. And he wasn't all that sure that he would like what it revealed.

But the process had started, and there was nothing he or anyone else could do to stop it.

Thirty-One

"Can you believe it was just a week ago that we walked through this door?" Robert asked Daniel as they headed up the stairs to the kitchen of the Ruby House.

They had waved at April, who was on the phone in the office. Daniel overheard something about the gallery and assumed she was discussing details with Seth. He knew they would begin working on the skylights today, and since April was the one designing the studio space, it made sense that they might need to check in with her.

Cindy had told the group at brunch the day before that the windows were in and Seth's crew would clear the gallery of debris so the painter could start painting in the morning. After that, they'd prepare the new exhibit and open again in a few days.

He had asked if he could help, but Cindy said there was already plenty of help. Daniel had been disappointed. He would have liked to be part of the process. He thought perhaps Cindy was trying to slow down what he felt was inevitable. Like it or not, they were going to end up more than friends.

Daniel thought maybe he could talk to Marsha and April about Cindy's hesitation. Was it about him, or was she just being careful? He had to admit he was a little worried about it, too. He didn't want to ruin his chances of staying in Spring Falls if something went wrong between the two of them.

In the kitchen, Daniel slid into the booth while Robert fetched the coffee, and he gazed out the window to observe Marsha and the yoga class. Marsha had mentioned that they would continue to hold the classes outdoors as long as the weather remained warm enough. Everyone seemed to prefer being outside, despite having access to the beautiful room at the front of the building.

"Maybe I should take yoga," Daniel said, watching how graceful everyone looked.

"Have you ever taken a yoga class?" Robert asked as he poured creamer into both their mugs. He knew how Daniel liked his coffee. A benefit of staying at his house for a few weeks.

"I haven't, but that looks like it would be good for me. I've noticed myself getting stiffer as I get older. Besides, it looks peaceful. Maybe I'll try her class sometime."

Robert set a cup of coffee on the table and slid into the booth opposite him.

"Are you thinking you are going to stay in Spring Falls for a while, then?"

"I guess I am. What about you?"

"I've been thinking about taking mom on a trip. You know me, it's hard to settle down. At least at the moment. I enjoy seeing things I never saw before, and mom has never had the chance to see the world."

"Have you asked her yet?"

Robert laughed. "I mentioned it to her, but I don't think she knew I was serious. I am, though. She'll change her mind."

"What will I change my mind about?" April asked, coming in to the kitchen.

"Coming with me on a trip."

"I didn't realize you were serious," April said, pouring herself a cup of coffee and sliding in the booth across from her son.

"Is he?" she asked Daniel.

"I believe he is."

"I'll think about it," April said, but in her mind, she was already making plans. What she was afraid to say out loud was how excited she was about the idea, because she just might break down in front of these two men.

Just her and Robert together. She couldn't begin to tell him how happy he had made her by asking. She would. But not at that moment.

"That was Cindy. She wanted to know if I would stop by her house, on the way to the studio, and get something she forgot. Would you two like to come with me?"

Robert winked at Daniel and they both said, "Sure!"

"Give me a few minutes, and we'll go."

Thirty minutes later, April was unlocking Cindy's door, explaining to Robert and Daniel that they all had keys to each other's houses, in case of emergencies or times like this.

Seeing the look on Daniel's face at being in Cindy's house, April told him he could look around if he wanted to. She had a few things to collect. Robert walked outside into the garden, still carrying his coffee.

"Maybe her art studio is open," April called out from the kitchen.

"Art studio?"

Coming out of the kitchen, holding a bag full of containers of food, she added, "Cindy thinks we don't know she still paints. But we do. We are just not sure why she doesn't show them. Perhaps you could look at them and convince her she should."

"I know little about paintings. It was my dad who was the painter."

"Still, let's look. She sometimes locks the studio, but maybe she left it open today."

Daniel shook his head. "If she locks the studio, maybe we shouldn't look."

"And maybe we should. Maybe you can tell me if she is right, that she is not an artist, because I think that's why she doesn't show them to us. She thinks she's not an artist. But if she is, perhaps you are the one who can pull her out of that belief."

Reluctantly, Daniel followed April upstairs. He wasn't sure this was a good idea. Would Cindy want them looking in her studio?

"It's not locked," she said, opening the door.

Daniel stepped in and then stopped breathing. There on the easel in the middle of the room sat one of his father's paintings.

"Not possible," he said, as he stepped in front of it. But in the left-hand corner were his father's initials. CJ. Cedric Jacobs.

Along the wall were painting of all sizes, all with their faces turned to face wall.

Almost too afraid to move, Daniel made himself turn one over. It was the same. Another of his father's paintings. Just like the ones in his father's back room. But even more beautiful.

"It can't be." Everything he had liked about Cindy was a lie. She was an art thief.

"What's wrong?" April asked as she watched Daniel's back grow rigid. "Aren't they any good?"

Through clinched teeth, Daniel whispered, "Exactly the opposite. A master painted these."

Then he walked down the steps and out the door.

"Daniel?" April called after him.

"Where's he going? What happened?" Robert asked, joining his mother at the door as she called after Daniel. They could see him running, already a few blocks away.

Daniel didn't realize he was running. He wasn't thinking at all. He wanted to be back in New York, with his lonely life, a life that didn't reveal horrible surprises. One where his father had not died and left him responsible. One where the woman he thought he had experienced love at first sight with was an art thief.

It was only when he had reached his apartment and thrown himself on the bed that he realized there was another explanation. One that made more sense.

It was his father who was the thief. But how could that be?

His phone was blowing up with texts from Robert.

"I'm okay. I need to sort something out," he finally texted back and then called Judith's office. Bruce said she liked figuring out mysteries. This was a big one, because it was very, very, personal.

Thirty-Two

"What happened?" Robert asked his mother again. He had tried texting Daniel, but he wasn't answering.

April shook her head. I made a mistake. I took Daniel into April's studio. It was unlocked, so I thought it was okay.

"She locks her studio?"

When Robert said those words, April realized Cindy had never wanted anyone to see the paintings. Why, she didn't know. But it was only then that April realized that it had been years since she had seen what Cindy had painted.

She had thought she had missed out because she hadn't been living in Spring Falls. But maybe that wasn't the reason. After all, she had been back for over a year, and still Cindy didn't talk about her art, let alone share it.

April racked her brain, trying to figure out just how long it had been since anyone last saw Cindy's paintings. She couldn't help but feel a sense of urgency in understanding the reasons behind that. The most pressing question on her mind was what could have possibly happened when Daniel saw them—she felt an increasing desperation to know the answer.

She had missed Daniel's reaction at first because she had been so struck by the beauty of the painting on the easel. At first she had thought that he was awestruck too, but then he had turned and his face was so white she thought he would pass out.

Thinking about what she had done, April backed up against the wall and slid down until she was sitting on the floor. What was she going to do?

"Mom, what's wrong?" Robert asked, sitting down beside her. He reached out and held her hand. It was icy cold.

"I think I betrayed my best friend."

"By seeing her paintings? How could that be a betrayal?"

"I don't know. That's the thing. I don't know, but I did somehow. Something happened when Daniel looked at the paintings. He looked scared and angry. What was Cindy hiding?"

Looking up at Robert, her blue eyes filled with tears, April asked, "What can I do? How can I fix this?"

Robert knew he could say it was nothing. But then that would be a lie. Something happened, something that meant a lot to Daniel, otherwise he wouldn't have bolted and run away.

But whatever it was, he would not let his mother take the blame for it. She had taken enough blame for other people's actions. And it didn't help when finally Daniel texted back that he was okay, when it was obvious he wasn't.

It was Cindy who was hiding something. And he was going to find out what it was.

• • • ● • ● • • •

Nancy took the call from Daniel. Judith was in her Monday morning meeting with all the accountants and bookkeepers that worked within her company. Checking Judith's appointment book, she told Daniel he could come in after lunch.

Hearing the panic in his voice, she asked if he would be okay. There was a long pause before he answered he would be.

At the apartment, Daniel paced the floor, trying to work out what he had seen. Cindy had his father's paintings in her art studio. It was impossible, of course. And he wished with all his heart that he hadn't looked, that he could turn back time and make a different decision. Why had he listened to April?

This was why he hesitated before doing anything. He was used to being betrayed by the world. His mother died, his father was a grade one jerk, the world was falling apart, and now he found out that a woman he actually liked was not who she appeared to be.

The question was, could he let it alone now? Did he really have to find out the truth? Couldn't he just walk away? He'd tell Steven to sell those paintings in his dad's studio. He'd leave town, call the police, and tell them about the stolen paintings.

The life he thought he might have in Spring Falls would not happen. They'd all hate him once he turned Cindy in. Hell, he'd hate himself.

The only tiny ray of hope was that there was another explanation, that it was his father who was the thief. However, both scenarios were completely improbable. And now that he found out Cindy's secret without her permission, would she hate him forever, even if she wasn't an art thief? As he stood in front of the paintings, he had believed that she was. Wouldn't that change her idea of him, and his idea of her forever, ruining their chance of happiness?

Looking at his watch, Daniel saw he had a few hours before his meeting with Judith. Should he go to the police station first? *No, he said to himself, No. It might not be what it seems. Do what you normally do. Stall. Wait it out.*

Realizing that he was going to explode with anxiety soon if he didn't do something, Daniel decided to go for a run. He could run through the woods and scream. He had a feeling the trees would forgive him for the noise, and perhaps he could gain some peace from them.

After all, think of all the things trees see and live through, Daniel thought, *but they still stand, trusting but alert, giving of themselves in every way possible.* Maybe he could be more like a tree if he stood there with them.

Wondering if he should change into running clothes, Daniel decided not to. There was only a brief window of time before he'd turn into a zombie, collapse onto the bed and become useless.

Strapping on his fanny back with his phone and money, taking a deep breath, Daniel stepped out the door and started running.

• • • ● • ● • • •

When April and Robert walked into the gallery, carrying the food she had asked them to bring, along with the notebook of sketches for the exhibit layout, Cindy knew something was wrong.

And the day had started so well, she thought.

But what she didn't know was that what happened was all about her. Why would she think that? Life was turning around. She had let go of being an artist herself. She was going to teach art classes. The studio already looked fantastic, even though it was a mess. And then there was Daniel. Perhaps finally she had found her one and only.

There was no way April and Robert's problem—because there was obviously a problem—would have anything to do with her.

It was only when April, who couldn't bring herself not to tell, said, "Daniel saw your paintings," that Cindy realized it was all about her. Daniel had seen the paintings, and that meant he knew her secret.

Thirty-Three

Emma rolled over in bed, glanced at the clock, and realized she had slept in. If she was in a regular school, she'd be late for school. Not for the first time, she was grateful that she wasn't. Homeschooling worked perfectly for her.

She could smell coffee and her mother moving around in the kitchen making breakfast. She had been doing that for the last three days. Yes, the first day her mother made breakfast, Emma had been out and her mother had thrown her breakfast away, but now that they had cleared the air between them, Emma had breakfast each day.

Which meant she hadn't gone running for two days. That would have to change. But it had been worth it. Saturday, she had coffee with Daniel, Bree, and Cindy. After coffee, Bree took her to meet Mary, Seth and baby Rho. Within minutes Emma had fallen in love with Rho, who she thought was the cutest baby ever born. Of course, she hadn't been around babies and other people much. Even so, Emma was sure that wouldn't change how much she had loved Rho at first sight.

That night she had babysat for Rho while Mary and Seth went out to dinner and the movies. They thanked her profusely afterwards and paid her well. So well that Emma wondered if Bree had told them more about her and her mother.

Of course, Mary worked with her mom, so she might have known a little already. Maybe her mother had shared some of their life with Mary. How would she know what her mother did when she was on her own?

After all, she had just learned that her mother wanted to be an artist, and her grandmother was one, too. Emma was sure she was missing huge chunks of information, but now she trusted that eventually she'd find out more.

It was another reason she hadn't gone running the last few days. Sunday morning she had stayed home and dallied over breakfast, hoping that her mom would tell her more. But she hadn't. Emma wanted to know everything right now. For fifteen years, her mother kept her in the dark. It was long past the time to be told the truth. But she told herself to be patient but persistent and eventually she'd learn the whole story.

"I have to work the lunch shift today," Veronica said during breakfast. "Do you want to come have lunch there? I could show you off to the rest of the staff, since you already met Mary. I think they would like to see the daughter I am always talking about."

"You talk about me?"

"Of course, I do. Don't you know how proud of you I am?"

And then, seeing Emma's face, took a deep breath, closed her eyes, and when she opened them again, Emma could see the sadness in them.

"You don't, do you?"

"It's okay, mom," Emma said, touching her mom's hand. "Now I do. And yes, that sounds fantastic. But do you mind if I go for a run after we do my lessons and before lunch?"

A few hours later, with her mother's blessing, Emma headed for the woods. Running later in the morning was different in town. Too many people. So she ran into the campus of the community college, where it was quieter since most of the students were in classes and then circled around towards the woods.

As she ran, she played her favorite game of imagination. One minute she was a fox, another she was a beam of light, and a few minutes later she was the wind as it rushed through the trees, making leaves rain down on her.

She'd been playing the game as long as she could remember, and loved how easy it was for her. People called it pretending, but for her it was imagining. Because if she could imagine it, wasn't it in some way real? She wasn't really sure if that was true, but as she studied more about quantum physics, she thought perhaps it was.

True or not, her imaginings fueled her desire to paint. To somehow bring to life what she felt and saw. Even though she could feel that it was her body moving through space, her feet hitting the ground, her breath flowing through her, it was just as easy for Emma to transform each leaf to a fairy that flew by her waving at her as it floated to the ground.

Although she was busy imagining, Emma also knew enough to keep herself aware while she ran. After all, she was a girl running alone, and in the woods. She had learned how to separate the part of her that was imagining and the part of her that was present in the real world. Despite that, when she heard the scream, she wasn't sure if it was her imagination or reality.

Either way, it scared her so much she stopped running and waited. There was nothing more. She decided she must have imagined it, even though it had sounded so real. Emma thought perhaps she should head home.

She heard a rustle of leaves before she saw him. Her first reaction was fear, and then she saw it was Daniel and relaxed.

He was looking down as he shuffled through the leaves, and hadn't seen Emma, so when she said, "Daniel," it startled him and he stepped back and tripped over a log.

"Are you alright?" she asked, rushing forward to help him up, and then seeing his face, added, "Wait, what's wrong?"

Daniel smiled at Emma, thinking she was like a fairy princess in the woods, coming to his rescue.

"Was that you that was screaming?"

"I thought the trees wouldn't mind."

"Well, they probably didn't, but it scared the crap out of me."

Then the two of them looked at each other, Daniel with leaves sticking to his pants, and started laughing.

After catching her breath, Emma asked, "Do you want to talk about it?"

Daniel shook his head.

"Are you hungry? I'm going to have lunch at ParaTi's. Want to come with me? You can meet my mom. I've told her about you, but she'd probably feel better if she knew you."

Brushing himself off, Daniel nodded, thinking that Emma would be a great way to keep his mind off of what he would have to talk to Judith about. Besides, Emma was right. If he was going to hang out with her, her mother should know who he was. And, yes, now that Emma asked, he realized he was starving.

"Can't think of anything I'd rather do."

"Walk or run?"

"Run," Daniel said, already heading out of the woods. Emma laughed and ran after him. "No, you don't, old man," and pulled ahead.

Emma slowed down after making her point and they walked the rest of the way to the restaurant to catch their breath before entering..

Emma waved at her mom and took Daniel over to meet her. "I found him in the woods," she explained.

Veronica shook hands with Daniel while Emma watched them with a smile, and Mary thought they all looked alike..

Daniel, shaking hands with Veronica, thought the same thing. He didn't know what it was about Spring Falls. He kept meeting people who felt familiar, and yet he was positive he had never met them before.

As he ate, Daniel thought about how different his life was from just a week before when he had eaten there on his own. That's when he realized why Veronica felt familiar. He had seen her then as she came in looking for a job.

Yep. That explains it, he thought to himself. *There was nothing mystical or magical going on. Just everyday life where you discover the woman you thought you could love might actually be an art thief. There was nothing magical about that at all.*

Thirty-Four

"Well, that explains it," Judith said after Daniel told her about what he had found at April's.

"Explains what?"

"Why April said she was going out of town for a few days."

Daniel stood up, almost knocking the chair over as he did.

"Wait, we need to get to her house to stop her from moving the paintings."

"Calm down, Daniel. Cindy isn't moving the paintings. She's going to visit some people out of town. She's looking for some craft pieces. That's their new exhibit, and she said they didn't have enough pieces yet. She went searching. She does that sometimes."

"But she could be lying. She could move the paintings. You said that explains it. If she isn't moving the paintings, what does it explain?"

"It explains why she is going herself rather than sending Mimi or Janet. You and April saw Cindy's paintings. I imagine she has to deal with that. She's been hiding them forever."

"What do you mean her paintings? Of course she has been hiding them. They are my father's paintings! The same paintings are in my father's studio."

"And you said the paintings in the studio were not what you expected your father to paint, didn't you?"

"I haven't seen my father for years. His old paintings weren't the same, but his initials were in the corner. Artists evolve. He got better."

"Or?"

"Or what?"

"Or there is another explanation, Daniel. I know Cindy. There is not a dishonest bone in her body. I know you barely know her, but even so, if you put Cindy beside your father and had to choose which one was the better person, which one would you choose?"

Daniel slumped down in his chair. All his anger deflated, and a deep sense of regret took its place. He had betrayed Cindy by choosing to believe she was an art thief without giving her a chance to explain. Of course, he'd choose Cindy in a heartbeat, even if she was an art thief. But if she wasn't, which seemed pretty apparent to him now, then why did she have his father's paintings?

Judith waited patiently, watching Daniel move through regret and then awareness.

"My father's paintings are really Cindy's? But how? And the initials?"

"Don't they both have the same initials? Cindy Jones, Cedric Jacobs. How long ago did your father start using those initials, because Cindy always has. Even when we were kids."

"I remember visiting his studio when I was about ten and looking at his paintings then and saw his initials in the corner. Before that, I don't remember seeing his paintings. Normally my mother and I would visit together for only a day, but that summer I stayed with my father for a few months."

"So, if we assume the paintings are Cindy's, the question is how did he end up with hers, not how did Cindy end up with his?"

Daniel leaned back in his chair, closed his eyes and took himself back to that summer. He barely remembered it. His father wouldn't let him leave the apartment while he taught his summer class.

The only reason he had seen his father's paintings that summer was because one day Cedric had let him watch the class. Maybe he thought he would want to become an artist too.

But everything about the studio made him want to run away. It was hot and stuffy. His father was lording it over everyone, screaming at the students one minute and fawning over them the next.

He couldn't believe that grownups let someone treat them that way. It was bad enough his father did it to him, but he was just a kid. The two men and two women in the studio just let it happen. He had felt sorry for them, and angry at the same time.

If they would only stop his father from ranting at them, maybe he would have the courage to stop his father himself. Later, he did, in a way. He told his mother he never wanted to spend time with his father that way again, and she had agreed.

Daniel remembered how heartbroken his mother had been when she discovered how he had spent those two months with his father.

"Daniel," Judith said, bringing him back from the past. He was unaware that he had started crying.

Judith moved over to sit beside him. "I'm sorry. Your father must have been a cruel man. But did you remember something?"

"I was remembering when I was ten. The last time I spent anytime with him. I realize now that even then I knew how crazy he was. And abusive. I guess I never allowed myself to fully process it."

Looking up at Judith, he said, "Four people were there. Two women and two men. I was just an immature kid, so I saw them as adults. But now I realize they were probably not that much older than me. I had a crush on one of the women that day. She was so beautiful. She smiled at me a few times, and I loved her for that."

"Did you see her paintings?"

Daniel closed his eyes, taking him back to that day. The heat, the yelling, the woman's sweet smile. He had glanced back at her as his father dragged him out after he complained how hot he was. She had waved at him, and then turned back to her painting.

"OMG," Daniel breathed out, the realization of who she was almost making him fall out of his chair.

"It was Cindy. That was Cindy!"

As Judith reached for her phone, Daniel felt as if his heart would burst out of his chest. He had fallen in love with Cindy all those years before, found her again, and then believed she was an art thief.

She wasn't an art thief. His father was. And for all these years, he had believed his father's life as an artist was true, as if it was real. And then, Cindy, poor Cindy, had believed his father too.

His father was the art teacher she had told him about. The man who had destroyed her belief in herself as an artist. And yet she had continued to paint beautiful master pieces anyway, but let no one see them.

"We have to find Cindy," he said, and then realized that Judith was already trying. And failing.

Thirty-Five

Cindy was halfway to Doveland when she realized she probably should have called Grace to let her know she was coming. However, she couldn't bring herself to do it. It had taken all her acting skills to convince Mimi and Janet that she had always planned to leave that afternoon.

Nevertheless, they had looked at her as if she had lost her mind. After April and Robert left, Cindy had told them she wanted to check out some artists in Doveland, but the suddenness of her decision had confused them.

"Where Grace lives? Where Rachel and Bryan live?" Janet had asked.

Mimi had simply stared at her, and Cindy knew why. Mimi didn't for a minute buy her story about needing to see some craft artists for their new exhibit. Cindy knew Mimi had sensed her unease as soon as April said that Daniel had seen her pictures, and knew Cindy's leaving that afternoon was her running away.

When April had said, "Daniel saw your paintings," it had felt as if her insides were being rearranged. Her heart had been beating so hard she thought for sure everyone could hear it. Daniel had seen her paintings and not said a word about them. It could only mean Daniel now knew what kind of artist she was and had decided he wanted nothing to do with her.

Sure, she already told him she wasn't an artist. But having the people she cared about actually see that for themselves was too much. So she had said the first thing she could think of, as if she had been planning it all along.

Well, in a way, she had been. Grace had invited her—well, all of them—to Doveland countless times since they met. Now, once again, something had happened in their lives because of Paul's letter to Bree before he died. That letter had started the entire process of the Ruby Sisters coming back together again, finding Bree's daughter, Bruce and Judith finding each other, and of course, meeting Grace.

Not for the first time, Cindy wondered how much Paul had foreseen how much his last gift to Bree would change all their lives.

But right now she couldn't face her life as it was, and she was taking Grace up on her offer to visit, even though Grace didn't know she was on her way. She was going, not because she wanted to visit Doveland, or find craft artists, but because she wanted—no, needed—to be some place no one knew her.

Well, Grace knows me, Cindy thought. *And Bryan and Rachel. But I can avoid them. Maybe I can hide in Grace's apartment, stay in bed all day and pretend that nothing has happened.*

All Cindy knew was that Grace owned a coffee shop in Doveland called Your Second Home. She knew that the coffee shop was located among the various shops surrounding the town's traffic circle. Cindy felt confident she could find it, and perhaps it would truly feel like a second home to her. Right now, she was desperate for a sense of belonging and comfort that such a place might provide.

Yes, she was running, but she was also running to someone she thought could help her. Grace would be an unbiased observer, and that is what she needed. Maybe she would want to see Rachel, after all. Rachel had come to Spring Falls with her husband Bryan a few times, so she knew she was comfortable with her. Maybe she'd find some peace in Doveland. Because right now she was furious with herself and felt as far from peaceful as she had ever been.

She had lied about her paintings and now she had left Mimi and Janet alone in the gallery to deal with the renovation. *What kind of person does that?* Cindy asked herself.

A few hours later, Cindy found the traffic circle and marveled at how beautiful the little park was that sat inside of it. She glimpsed the coffee shop and parked in front of it.

She sat in the car thinking she could just keep driving, but despite the mixed cocktail of sick fear, longing, anger, and sorrow that rolled around inside of her, Cindy knew she was in the right place.

• • • ● • ● • • •

Grace almost dropped the plate of muffins she was delivering to a table tucked into the corner of her shop when she saw who had walked through the door.

Quickly setting the muffins down, she practically ran to the door, embracing Cindy in a hug. Stepping back, she inspected Cindy's face and pointed upstairs.

"It's unlocked. Go on up. I'll be there in a sec."

The coffee shop was almost empty. It was nearing dinner, and only a few regular customers were sitting at their tables, tapping away at something on their computers.

Grace knew that a few of them were writing books, and she was still playing with the idea of marketing their books in a section of her bookstore as "Books Written at Your Second Home."

Motioning to her barista, she explained she had a friend arrive, and she was leaving her in charge.

As she headed upstairs, Grace wondered if she should cancel the regular Monday night meeting of the women's council, or if the fact that Cindy had arrived at that moment meant it was perfect timing.

Looking at Cindy's face as she headed upstairs without a word, Grace decided it was part of the universe's plan to bring Cindy to Doveland on that day. Grace knew Cindy would understand and relate to a gathering of women who solved things together. After all, Cindy had the Ruby Sisters.

Why Cindy hadn't turned to the Ruby Sisters in this moment, Grace didn't know. But the council would find out and do whatever it took to help. After all, their circle of women had been solving problems, finding solutions, and helping people for years right here in this living room.

And they'd do it again. Besides, she couldn't wait for Cindy to meet Valerie, Emily, and Ava. Cindy had already met Rachel. They'd listen to what was going on and help sort out the problem for her.

Opening the door to her apartment, Grace found Cindy staring out at the park inside the traffic circle. A few people were sitting on the benches, and someone was inside the gazebo drinking coffee while reading a book. Memories of the many things that had happened in that park flashed by, and she sighed.

Grace put her arm around Cindy and Cindy let herself lean in, thinking that Grace was the perfect name for this woman. She had come to the right place.

She needed help, and this was where she was going to get it.

Thirty-Six

"She's with Grace," Judith told everyone gathered at Cindy's studio.

"Oh, thank God," April said and sank back into the couch in the writer's room. They could hear the construction crew upstairs finishing up for the day. Seth had come down earlier and said they were almost done, and the group of friends were waiting for them to leave before getting down to the business at hand. Which was determining why Cindy had left without warning.

All the Ruby Sisters were present, along with Mimi, Janet, Robert, Daniel, Bruce, and Booker. Judith looked around the room and wondered how their circle had expanded so much. The room was small, but it held them all, and was perfect for the discussion they needed to have.

Once the crew had gone, Judith turned to Daniel and asked him to tell them what happened, since all of it revolved around him, and not everyone had heard the full story.

Daniel took a deep breath. Only a week ago, he had met none of these people. He couldn't remember the last time he had been in such a small room with so many people in it. He had chosen a life on his own. If it wouldn't have been for Robert, it probably would have stayed that way. So, even though he was overwhelmed and afraid, he started out by thanking Robert for recognizing his distress the day he saw him in the coffee shop, and then inviting him to come to Spring Falls with him.

"If you wouldn't have basically forced me to come with you," Daniel started, and then when Robert protested, added, "well, forced me out of my chosen path of withdrawal which was getting me nowhere, I wouldn't have met Cindy, all of you, and realized what my father had done."

Mimi and Janet looked at each other and smiled. They had recognized the look Daniel had given Cindy, and made a bet with each other that something had happened between them, even if the two of them weren't aware of it. Now it appeared that at least Daniel knew.

Booker stood off in the corner behind Bree's chair. He had something to add to the story, but there was no point in telling them all until Daniel explained the situation.

For the next thirty minutes, Daniel explained what they had found. He told them about his father and the paintings he had discovered in the back room after his father died. Paintings that made him wonder if he had ever known his father. The answer was yes and no. He had always known his father as controlling and selfish, and a decent artist. At least good enough that he had made a living selling his work and teaching master classes.

What he hadn't known, and still didn't totally understand how it happened, was that his father had not painted the paintings Daniel had discovered in the back room.

"Then who did?" Bree asked. She hadn't even known that Cindy had left town at the last minute. Bree was trying to catch up with what had happened.

"We are still confirming what I think is true. My father's art dealer, Steven, will be in town in the morning, and we'll know for sure then, but I believe Cindy painted them."

April jumped in then, reminding them that none of them had seen any of Cindy's paintings since she had gone to New York to study with a master. Cindy had opened an art gallery but never once shown any of her paintings.

"We all knew she was painting, though," Marsha pointed out.

"Yes, but did anyone ever see them?" April asked.

"No," Judith answered, "And we should have asked why. I should have asked why. After all, it was me here with her all the years you were all not living here. We had coffee meetings almost every Monday morning. How did I not notice?"

"And I stayed at her house for months and didn't notice. She locked her art room, for heaven's sake," Marsha added.

"There is no reason to blame yourself," Daniel said. "It was my father who is to blame. It was my father she went to study with. She told me she had studied with a master but didn't mention his name. But she confessed he convinced her she wasn't an artist. She believed him, and from then on, she acted as if what he said was real."

"Your father?" Marsha said, once again marveling at how the universe brought everything together. In this case, in order to fix what had been broken so many years before.

"Yes. Strange, isn't it? But what I think happened is he made her leave the paintings that she did while she was there with him, telling her they were worthless. But this morning, April let me into Cindy's studio and I saw what she had been painting since then.

"The works that my father kept are beautiful, and Steven has been trying to get me to sell them for a lot of money. But the ones in Cindy's studio are stunning. Over the years, she had gotten better and better."

"So," April broke in, "when Cindy found out we had seen her paintings, she freaked out. She must have thought that now we knew for sure she wasn't really an artist, confirming what she had believed about herself all along."

"Which is why she left town," Mimi added, thinking out loud. "Right in the middle of building her art studio, something she would never do unless she was really upset."

"Yes, because we never had time to tell her that the paintings were beautiful, or what my father had done. In fact, until now, I was worried that it was the other way around. That Cindy had stolen my father's art." Daniel dropped his head and mumbled, "Not sure I'll ever be able to make that up to her."

"Well, there is a lot of misinformation going around," Judith said. "To repeat myself, no one is to blame except for your father, Daniel. He took away Cindy's belief in herself, and we can be grateful that she kept painting, even though she thought she was failing at it."

"Shouldn't we let her know what we have found?" April said.

"Well, we are not entirely sure yet. I think we need to wait for the dealer's opinion. We'll be violating Cindy's privacy again, but this time, for her own good," Judith answered. "Grace and her friends will give Cindy all the support she needs right now. We'll find out exactly what happened and if Cindy hasn't come home by then, one of us will go get her."

Everyone nodded, not sure what else they could do.

Booker cleared his throat. "There is another problem, though. I got a call today from the detective investigating Daniel's father's death. Turns out, they discovered Cindy was in town the day Cedric died. They'd like to talk to her."

Thirty-Seven

Robert insisted Daniel spend the night at his mother's house with him. He had an inkling of how Daniel felt and Robert knew it was best Daniel wasn't alone, no matter how much he wanted to be.

When Robert had found out that his father was a serial killer, he felt as if he, and the world he had known, had shattered into pieces and he was no longer part of anything he had known before. Although he still wasn't completely put back together, but he was getting better every day. He and his world were not the same as they were before, but in so many ways, his life was better now.

However, Robert knew that what had happened to him differed from what Daniel was now experiencing. He had never had an inkling of what his father had been doing, and Daniel had always known that his father was a terrible man. Not a serial killer, but a killer of people's spirits.

But learning that Cedric was an art thief took away the one thing Daniel had thought was true about his father. His father wasn't an artist at all. Or at least not a good one. Instead, he was a con man. And that he had somehow conned Cindy made it worse. Although

Daniel had shared none of his feelings about what he had learned, no one had missed the pain and sorrow that radiated out from him.

Bad fathers, Robert thought. *That's what Daniel and I have in common, and we didn't even know it.* He thought perhaps they had unconsciously recognized that commonality, and it was why they became friends.

And then Daniel met Cindy, and Robert had been delighted to see the spark in Daniel's eyes. He wasn't sure he had ever seen that before. Robert had thought that finally Daniel could build a life for himself. He could see Daniel settling down in Spring Falls and finding happiness with Cindy.

All that changed now, though. Daniel had seen Cindy's art, and Cindy had run away. And then they learned the police wanted to question Cindy about being in New York when Cedric died. It was just routine, but still terrifying, and Daniel, on hearing the news, looked like someone had punched him in the gut.

Robert smiled to himself, thinking about the reaction of all Cindy's friends when Booker had told them what the New York police wanted with Cindy. No one in that room believed that Cindy had anything to do with Cedric's death. A man like that had made many enemies. Perhaps one of them was responsible, but definitely not Cindy.

Before Robert had come to Spring Falls, his mother had told him about Judith and how her hair seemed to light up when she was angry. He thought she was exaggerating, but then he saw it for himself. It was amazing. Impossible, of course, but there it was. Every one in the room had reacted in their own way, but everyone agreed it was not possible that Cindy had anything to do with Cedric's death.

However, it was Judith who had stood up and said, "No. Cindy is the victim in this, and we are going to prove it together."

After confirming that Steven would be in town the next day, Judith told everyone to go home and get a good night's sleep.

They wouldn't do Cindy any good if they were all exhausted from worrying.

"We've met bigger challenges than this together," Judith said. "Besides, how many other young artists' lives did Cedric Jacobs ruin? This has nothing to do with Cindy."

It was Judith who had suggested to Robert that he should take Daniel home with him. Marsha and his mother had agreed. Daniel had said no, but his mother said she wouldn't take no for an answer, and that was the end of that.

Robert had taken Daniel to his apartment to pick up a few things, not leaving him alone for a minute. He knew how easy it would have been for Daniel to just lie down on the bed and hate himself all night. That would not happen on his watch.

When Daniel protested that there was no place for him to sleep at the Ruby House, Robert reminded him that there was a couch that turned into a bed in the guest bedroom. They had lived together for a few weeks in an apartment in New York, which wasn't much bigger than that room. A few nights would be nothing.

But hours later, no one was sleeping yet. Marsha was downstairs in the studio trying to calm herself by doing yoga. April was in her bedroom, trying to read. Daniel was in the backyard, sitting in a chair, and Robert felt as if he was guarding them all. It was the least he could do. He hadn't been there for his mother before, but he was now. Whatever happened, he would be the kind of son and friend he had always wanted to be.

Thirty-Eight

Once everyone else had gone, Booker, Judith, Bree, and Bruce stayed in the writer's room before heading home. The atmosphere was laden with anxiety, just like the dust from the renovations that clung to every surface. Each of them silently acknowledged their worries, yet no one spoke them out loud. Even Mittens was upset. He was huddled under the sofa and no one could get him to come out.

Mimi and Janet had been the last to leave, checking everything in the gallery and the studio to make sure it was buttoned up for the night. Everyone knew what they were really doing was trying to make sense of what had happened. If they could take care of the gallery, maybe they could take care of Cindy.

After making sure Judith had her key, they left through the back door, locking it behind them. As the lock clicked, Booker cleared his throat, breaking the heavy silence in the room. His eyes darted around the room, studying each person's face. He knew they were all thinking the same thing. How were they going to find out the truth?

"What do you think?" Judith asked. "Is there something we don't know?"

"There is a lot we don't know," Booker said. "We don't know why Cindy was in New York. And we only have a ten-year-old boy's memory of Cindy being in Cedric's class that summer.

"We really know very little about Cedric's life. We know he wasn't a good father or husband. But what else do we know? Has he really done things that would make someone want to kill him? From what we do know, it seems entirely possible. It can't be just Cindy that he mistreated."

Bruce leaned forward in his chair and said, "I know that trust seems well set up and fairly uncomplicated. Cedric left everything to Daniel. There's a decent amount of money, plus his paintings and his studio in New York. He rented his apartment and Daniel said he cleared that out before leaving New York. What he didn't give away, or sell, is now in the studio.

"The trust doesn't mention any other children. It's Daniel who believes that his father must have a few, knowing his father's predilection for young women. Daniel wants to find them and share his father's wealth with them. Is this because Daniel is a nice guy? Or does he feel guilty that he was the only one recognized as Cedric's heir? Either way, Judith's internet wizard Matt is searching for other children of Cedric. But even if we find other children, it's doubtful they have anything to do with all of this."

"Doesn't that make him a predator? Young women. Did they agree to have sex with him? Or did he con them? And if he copied artists and sold the works as his own, doesn't that make him an art thief?" Bree asked.

"Unless he actually sold a painting that was Cindy's, or copied what she did directly, he could have claimed he was only doing what all artists do—imitating other artists and then making something of their own from that.

"Yes, Cedric went overboard, but Daniel said the paintings his father hadn't sold were much better than the ones he had been selling as his. So those unsold paintings are probably Cindy's. So it's obvious Cedric wasn't capable of reproducing Cindy's work exactly."

"He still made a lot of money from imitating them," Bree protested.

Booker ran his hand through his hair before answering. "But again, unless he sold Cindy's paintings as his, he did nothing illegal. And maybe Cindy gave him those paintings."

"Well, if she did, it was because he conned them from her," Judith said.

"Did she?"

"I don't know. I spoke to Grace and told her everything that was happening here. She said that she and her friends would take good care of Cindy, and if Cindy shares anything relevant, Grace will get back to me."

Judith sighed, thankful that Grace was helping Cindy but wishing that she hadn't run off. It bothered her that Cindy had never talked to her about her paintings. But it bothered her even more that she hadn't asked her why she hadn't let her see any of her work for all these years. What kind of friend had she been?

"I'm still going through Cedric's record keeping. So far, nothing stands out as illegal. Sloppy bookkeeping, but most people's records look like his. I'll find out more from the art dealer when he arrives in the morning."

"I don't think we can do more until then," Booker said, unconsciously reaching for Bree's hand as they stood.

They had already planned to spend the night together at Bree's. Addie was waiting at Bree's house for them to come home. It was still warm enough for Addie to be outside in Bree's yard, but she was probably getting hungry. He knew he was.

Booker sighed, thinking about Cindy. She was the one who always took care of everyone. She was the one who had gone to Bree when Bree's husband Paul died. It was always Cindy who leaned in and helped when anyone was upset.

It was completely out of character for Cindy to have done anything wrong. But what Booker hadn't yet told the group was he was supposed to get a statement from Cindy and if what she told him didn't clear her, a detective would arrive from New York to question her further. If all that didn't go well, it would be him who would have to arrest her.

He was determined that before things got that far, they'd find out what really happened, and clear Cindy's name. She was the one who needed help this time, and she probably wasn't even aware of it. She had run because she thought they had discovered that she wasn't an artist and she was ashamed that she had hidden that fact from them.

Cindy didn't know how untrue that was. She didn't know that Cedric had lied to her, and possibly stolen from her.

But what worried Booker was that all of that was an act. That Cindy had found out about Cedric. That she had sought revenge against him, or tried to get her paintings back and something had gone wrong. There was enough confusion about what had happened to make it appear as if she was the one who had done something wrong, and she had fooled them all.

For the Ruby Sisters' sake, he prayed that wasn't true. Cindy could stay away for the day, but she needed to come back soon and make things right.

Thirty-Nine

Grace was thinking the same thing as Booker and Judith. She'd have to make sure Cindy got back to Spring Falls soon. Judith had explained the situation to her, and she realized that the longer Cindy stayed away, the more guilty she would look. They needed to clear up what had happened as soon as possible.

But looking at Cindy, Grace knew she needed to rest first. She had taken Cindy to the guest bedroom and suggested she get some sleep before dinner, not telling her about the women that were coming over later.

Cindy protested she hadn't come to take naps.

"After you rest, we'll talk, and you can tell me all about why you are here. But right now, would you make much sense?"

Cindy looked around the room and let herself feel her exhaustion. It had been creeping up on her for years. It felt as if every painting stacked against her wall had taken something out of her, and now that everyone knew she was a fraud, she felt completely drained.

"You're right. I need a little nap, if you don't mind."

A few hours later Cindy woke to the sound of voices, and she could smell something cooking.

After straightening her clothes and brushing her hair off her face, she made her way to the living room. When she saw there was a group of women milling around the kitchen and living room, she turned to go back to the bedroom.

But Rachel saw her coming, jumped up, hugged her, whispering that they were all there for her.

"I can't do this, Rachel. I can't talk to all of you, whoever they are."

"They are all my friends. We are like your Ruby Sisters. Let us help."

Cindy nodded in agreement. After all, what other options did she have? She had fled to this place, and running elsewhere seemed futile. Besides, confiding in a group of strangers might prove helpful, and she had nothing to lose by sharing her story.

Rachel introduced her to each woman, starting with Ava Anders. She explained it was Ava and Grace who had first come to Doveland and gathered the rest of the women once they moved here. Ava's blue eyes were warm and understanding as she shook Cindy's hand.

Next Grace introduced her to Valerie Price. "Valerie lives right across the street. She's the person who knows everyone in town. Her husband was one of the people that Ava knew who moved here after they did. He's the town's doctor. Valerie has lived here the longest. She owns an Interior Design company. The beauty of all our homes, and even this town, has a lot to do with Valerie."

Valerie blushed as she shook Cindy's hand and added, "These women saved my life… in more ways than one. I'm glad you're here. We've heard about you and your gallery. Perhaps we can do some things online together?"

Cindy's eyes filled with tears, already feeling that she had come to the right place to get help.

Then Grace led Cindy to a tall young woman with long blond hair. "Cindy this is Emily Sands. You two have a lot in common. Emily runs an art school/retreat out on the mountain. It started with just dance, but now includes writing and art."

"Perhaps you could come spend some time here next summer and teach a class," Emily said. "We would love to have you."

"But you don't know me," Cindy protested.

All the women laughed, including Grace.

"Yes, we do," Emily answered. "Grace shared how she met you all, and Rachel has kept us up to date with some of your adventures in Spring Falls."

At first Cindy wondered if it should offend her that Grace and Rachel had talked about them, and then realized that was absurd. When she went home, she'd share with her friends about people she met in Doveland. Besides, that meant they knew enough that she didn't need to explain the situation.

I just need to tell the truth, Cindy said to herself.

Out loud she answered, "Then I would love to teach at your art center next summer!" She didn't add, *if everything works out.*

Cindy thought how much this group was like the Ruby Sisters at home. Instead of pizza, they had spaghetti, but the feeling was the same. They were women who had supported each other through thick and thin.

As they sat down to dinner, piling heaps of spaghetti onto her plate and adding a piece of garlic bread, Cindy understood why she had come to Doveland. It was a place where no one had a stake in the outcome of what she was and what she had done. She could tell them the story, and they would listen, ask the right questions, and help her decide what to do about the mess she had made. Then she could go back to Spring Falls and deal with her life. Sort it out. Make it right.

Cindy allowed herself to be enveloped by the warmth and camaraderie of the women of Doveland, their fascinating tales of adventure captivating her and making her own life seem dull in comparison. Yet, as they inquired about her own experiences, she smiled to herself.

Her life hadn't been dull at all. It was simply a matter of perspective. Each individual's journey held its own unique depth and allure, hers included, and she found solace in that awareness.

What Cindy didn't know was that when she returned, she would be questioned about the murder of Cedric Jacobs, and since she didn't have an alibi for when it happened, she would be the chief suspect in his death.

Forty

"I think I am going to go take Marsha's yoga class this morning," Emma announced to her mother. They had just finished breakfast, which meant once again that Emma had not gone running.

It had been a conscious decision on Emma's part to stay home again. She had decided that she didn't have to run every day, or she could run later, because now that her mother worked the lunch and dinner shift at ParaTi's, it meant they had less time together.

Although Emma didn't understand why they needed money now when they hadn't before, Emma figured if her mother was willing to work that hard and let her take art classes, she should be willing to be more present at home. The tension between the two of them had eased, and although her mother didn't know it, a lot of Emma's diminishing resentment had come about because of Daniel.

When Daniel had shared a little about his father, Emma had realized that although things weren't perfect, her mother tried hard to be a good mother. Not like Daniel's father, who had never tried and sounded like a horrible man.

So that morning after announcing she was thinking about going to yoga, Emma had surprised them both by asking her mother, "Do you want to come with me?"

Afraid to ask Emma why she asked her to come with her in case that would make her change her mind, Veronica said, "Absolutely, just give me a minute to change."

Glancing at her phone, Emma said, "It starts in thirty minutes," and sat down on the floor by her yoga bag and mat to wait and think about how her life was changing. For one thing, she was looking forward to being in the Ruby House.

The first time she had seen the sign over the door that said, "Joy Lives Here," she thought it was stupid, and it annoyed her to think someone would believe such a thing.

But every time she went to a dance class, she felt a little more of what the sign meant. She realized that the sign didn't just mean that joy only lived in that house, but it could live in people too. And to her surprise, had felt that joy inside of her.

And that was because of April and Marsha. Both of them made everyone feel welcome at the Ruby House, and Emma could see that joy lived in them.

Which was amazing because Emma, like everyone else in Spring Falls, knew April and Marsha's stories, so if anyone might feel angry and resentful about life, it would be them. Instead, they had joy inside of them and she wondered how hard it had been for them to become that way.

As Emma waited for her mother, she thought about how, when she let joy live inside of her, there was less room for resentment and worry. Maybe those two emotions couldn't be in the same place at the same time.

So each time Emma went to class, she was a little less angry, and as her resentment faded, she could admit that she did love to dance. Especially when she let herself imagine dance as making art in space instead of on a canvas. Instead of painting with a paintbrush, she made shapes with her body. Flowing with the music, she could feel the same way that flowing with the shapes she made on the canvas felt to her.

Besides, Marsha was a fantastic teacher. Although Marsha expected them to do each movement better each time they did it, somehow she did that by being both kind and stern at the same time. Marsha explained that each exercise in ballet was both a stretch and strength exercise that complimented each other. What appeared to be two opposing forces actually needed to work together.

"Strength without flexibility is not actually strength. It's a weakness. In life and in dance," Marsha had said, and Emma had thought then that Marsha was speaking from experience.

So when Marsha had invited her to come to morning yoga, Emma had said she would think about it.

"Just come when you are ready," Marsha had said. But when she added that the classes were outside for a few more weeks, that had made it sound even better to Emma.

So I guess I'm ready now, Emma thought, as her mother came out of the bedroom looking nervous. Which Emma realized was exactly how she felt.

• • • ● • ● • • •

Daniel had tried to sleep, but eventually got up, and not wanting to disturb anyone, quietly made himself a cup of coffee and headed down to the dance studio.

The curtains were open and the full moon shone through the leaves of the maple tree out front, making shifting shapes on the polished wood floors. As he sipped the hot coffee, Daniel watched the moonlight dance on the floor and thought about his father and Cindy.

He thought back to that summer when he had first seen Cindy. As a ten-year-old boy, it was impossible to believe that the beautiful twenty-year-old woman would ever notice him. But she had smiled and waved.

But after all this time, without remembering they had met before, she had noticed him again and now the ten years' difference in their age meant nothing. Now Daniel understood why he had felt that he had known Cindy before. He admired her from afar as he stood watching his father berate the four people in the room who had wanted to please him.

Including Cindy, who he remembered had stared at his father as if he was a minor god. Always back to his father. Who his father was and what he had done to others was the problem. All the lives he had ruined by telling lies. All the women who had affairs with him because of his charisma and because they believed he was an art master and could make or break their careers.

Now he knew it had been his father who had told Cindy she wasn't a talented artist, and she had believed what he said all these years, as if anything his father said was true.

As Daniel thought back over that summer, how he knew his father was having another affair, because his mother had warned him about his father, he thought about Cindy and the other woman in the studio.

And for the first time, it occurred to Daniel that Cindy might have been the woman he was having an affair with.

No, he said to himself. *No.* But the thought had taken root. And if that was true, and if Cindy had found out that his father had lied and been copying her work all these years, would that have been enough to make her want to kill him?

It was enough to make him feel that way.

No, he said to himself again, *No. Cindy would never do such a thing no matter how angry she might be.*

Daniel finished his coffee, and setting the cup beside him, closed his eyes and let himself drift back to that summer, and his first sighting of Cindy Jones.

A few hours later, Marsha found him there, slumped up against the wall.

Waking him up, she told him people would arrive for morning yoga in a few minutes.

"I'm not taking no for an answer. You are taking yoga this morning. I have a mat for you. Let's go."

A few minutes later, when Emma and Veronica stepped outside on the deck, Emma felt another surge of joy when she saw Daniel sitting on a mat near the house.

Daniel felt the same thing. Which surprised him. All he knew was that when he saw Emma and her mother, he felt as if he already knew them, and their presence made him happy.

For now, that had to be enough for him because there was nothing else he could do while they waited for Cindy to come home.

Forty-One

Steven Binot drove his rental car down the main street of Spring Falls, parked in front of the first coffee shop he saw, and stepped out into a beautiful late September morning.

He could smell the leaves that were turning, and the air was crisp and refreshing. Young people staring at phones walked by, reminding him that Daniel had told him that Spring Falls had a community college.

He watched as one of the young men stubbed his toe on a large pot filled with colorful flowers. Steven thought they might be zinnias. He remembered them from his mother's garden.

It was a wide sidewalk, so it wasn't the plants' fault that the boy almost dropped his phone and then glared at the pot as if it had no right to be there. Steven laughed to himself. The inattention of the screen-fed generation to the world around them was not really a laughing matter, but seeing the boy huff off over such a small thing, he couldn't help it.

Daniel had told him it was a pretty town and although he was partial to big cities like New York, Steven had to agree. Main Street appeared to be filled with charming small shops and restaurants.

Trees and flowers lined the wide sidewalks. He knew the art gallery was only a few blocks away. With lots of foot traffic in town, Steven expected the stores did well.

Normally, Steven wouldn't drive to see a client. They came to him. But this time, he was making an exception. He had sold Cedric Jones' painting for years because there was always a market for them. He had admired the paintings and was grateful that they sold so well, but after Cedric's death, when he saw the paintings hidden in the back room, he knew those paintings were much more valuable. And like Daniel, he wondered if he had ever known Cedric.

The paintings in the back room were beautiful with a depth he had never seen in Cedric's painting before. They were luminescent, alive with an internal beauty, which was not something he would have ever said about Cedric's paintings.

So when Daniel called and told him they were probably not Cedric's, it didn't surprise him. But if they weren't Cedric's, why did he have them? Were they copies of someone else's paintings? If so, he had been doing it for years, because they were the same style that Cedric had painted for as long as he had represented him.

Now, Steven was glad that Daniel had insisted on not selling those paintings, because if they weren't Cedric's—well, he didn't want to think about what would have happened once the truth had come out.

As an art dealer, Steven dealt with all kinds of people. Some were kind and generous, others were cheap, angry, inconsiderate, and rude. Cedric fell into the latter group. He had never liked Cedric. But liking someone was not a requirement for doing business in the art world with them. If he had to like everyone, he would have very few clients.

And since Cedric was one of the most self-centered people he had ever met, he expected there were many people who would have wanted to kill him. So even though at first his death might have looked like suicide, Steven knew eventually they would realize it wasn't. Cedric's ego was too big to intentionally kill himself.

Once the police declared Cedric's death a murder, Steven reviewed the long list of people who hated Cedric Jacobs, who in a moment of rage might have done it. He hoped that the woman he had come to town to meet wouldn't be considered the killer, although the cynic in him thought that would make the paintings even more valuable. And after all, if she had discovered what Cedric had been doing, maybe she felt like killing him.

However, he had not come to town to solve a murder. He had come to confirm that it wasn't Cedric who was the artist behind those paintings. And then he had to confirm that it was the woman Cindy Jones instead. Daniel was quite insistent that they were her paintings. But he had to see it for himself.

In fact, he wanted to see her paint. It was how, back in 1986, a Hawaiian court confirmed that it was Margaret Keane who was the artist who painted the children with enormous eyes. not her husband, Walter, as he claimed.

Men were always claiming credit for things that women did, Steven thought to himself. His mother raised him differently than that, and if that was what Cedric Jacobs had been doing all these years, he would make sure that the truth came out. But if he only copied the idea of the paintings, it wasn't technically a crime.

The question was, why did Cindy Jones not show her work? After all, she had her own art gallery. She could have been selling them for years.

Did Cedric threaten her? Or convince her she had no talent? Either scenario wouldn't surprise Steven. Cedric ruined more artists' belief in themselves than he could count.

After coffee, Steven thought he'd drive, or maybe walk. to the art gallery and look around before he introduced himself. He'd just be a stranger in town and get a feel for the place before anyone knew who he was.

But his introduction to the gallery didn't happen that way. He didn't remain a stranger long because it was Judith who saw the tall man with curly gray hair and the fashionable short gray beard step out of the car. He had on a sports coat over jeans that looked expensive and some kind of tennis shoe. She figured they were expensive, too.

She recognized him from the publicity picture she had found on the internet. This was the man who would confirm who painted the pictures. That what he said could either break Cindy's heart or fulfill her childhood dream convinced Judith that she should step up and introduce herself. She would not leave Cindy's future to chance.

So before he even got to the coffee shop, Judith had crossed the street and walked up to him. Steven had seen her coming. She was hard to miss. Tall, elegant, with flaming red hair. At first, he thought she was heading for someone else and turned to look around to see who it could be.

But she called his name, and he realized it was him she was heading for. He wasn't sure if that was a good thing or not, but it was apparent that she knew who he was, so he was trapped.

An hour later, after coffee, and a grilling by Judith about his work, Judith led Steven to the art gallery.

Mimi and Janet came out to meet him, and Mimi was so good at pitching him that Steven didn't realize what she had been doing until he agreed to let some of his artists show their work there.

Impressive, Steven thought as he looked at the facilities. He saw the almost finished studio space where the lessons would be, checked out the writers' room, and then was given a brief tour of their online presence.

"And when can I see Cindy's paintings?" Steven asked after being shown everything, including the storage room hidden behind the walls of the gallery.

"None of her paintings are here," Judith said. "You'll have to wait until Cindy comes home to see them."

"And that will be when?"

"Later today, or first thing in the morning. You can stay at my house, though. I have a few guest rooms, or you could stay at my fiancé's house. He's the one who had been looking over the will and the trust Cedric set up."

As Judith called Bruce to let him know she was bringing Steven over and he would stay there, she giggled to herself.

She knew that Mimi and Janet were now barely containing themselves. She had thrown the news out that she and Bruce had decided to marry as if it was nothing, and yet, it was everything.

As Judith led Steven out the front door, she looked back at Janet and Mimi and gave them both a big grin. They just stood there, looking stunned.

Judith wondered how long it would take before everyone knew. She thought maybe a day. However, when she walked into her office an hour later and Nancy looked up at her and smiled so wide Judith wondered if her face would crack open, Judith knew it was over. Everyone knew. Now she'd have to tell the story. She was looking forward to it.

Forty-Two

"Well," Nancy huffed, standing up at her desk, hands on her hips, looking both stern and delighted at the same time. Judith had to laugh at the sight.

Nancy was barely five feet tall, and probably weighed less than a hundred pounds, but when she wanted to be intimidating, she was. It was one reason Judith had hired her. Nancy West was kind and efficient, but blunt and not afraid of her, and that's what she wanted in an assistant.

Judith knew she didn't need someone who agreed with her all the time. She needed push back. That's how she discovered new ideas and solved problems. And push back was what Nancy was giving her.

Nancy stood there—her blond bob, tipped with purple inspired by Janet's ever changing hair color, shining from the sun coming in the front window, trying not to smile—and projected the 'why didn't I know and you should have told me' look.

"Yes, it's true," Judith said.

Nancy dropped all pretensions of upset and launched herself at Judith. For once Judith allowed herself to be hugged by the elf-like

Nancy, doing her best to hug her back, although it felt as if she was hugging a child.

The two of them rarely exchanged outward affection, and they normally kept their private lives separate, but since Nancy also answered Bruce's office phone, she was part of both their lives. This marriage would affect her, too.

Nancy reached out and held up Judith's left hand. "No ring?"

"No ring. Not necessary. We have better places to put that kind of money."

Seeing Nancy's face, she added, "Yes, I'll wear a wedding ring."

When Judith's next client came in the door, Nancy turned to greet him, and became the efficient manager of Judith's office again. But Judith knew Nancy wanted all the details, and she probably deserved to get them.

After taking her client into her office, Judith stepped back out into the waiting room and asked Nancy if she could call all the Ruby Sisters, and Mimi and Janet, and have them come to her house that night so she and Bruce could share the news officially.

"And you come too, Nancy," she added.

When Judith stepped back into her office, Nancy stared at the closed door, wondering if the earth had tilted on its axis. She'd never been invited to one of Judith's gatherings before. *It makes sense that I am this time,* she thought. *After all, I work for them both.* Even so, it was unprecedented.

After a moment's pondering over the changing events, Nancy started making phone calls, telling them as little as possible, just that Judith had news to share.

Of course, everyone but Cindy already knew what the news was all about. But they were all excited about having a chance to find out all the details. When Bree asked if she could bring Booker, Nancy had to make the decision to say yes. After all, he and Bruce were honorary members of the Ruby Sisters. Then April asked if Daniel and Robert could come, and Nancy said yes, hoping that she was doing the right thing. The little gathering was turning into a bigger event.

Judith will probably be okay with this, Nancy thought. She loved having people over. Then, although Judith didn't tell her to order pizzas, Nancy did anyway. She had ordered pizzas enough times for the group to know how many and what kind to get.

At the last minute Nancy remembered to call Bruce and tell him what was happening, grateful she had dodged a bullet on that one. *Imagine having an engagement celebration without the groom*, she thought.

Bruce had laughed, saying he had already heard from clients that they had heard he was engaged. News traveled fast in Spring Falls. Then he reminded Nancy that the art dealer, Steven, was staying with him, so he'd have to come too.

After talking to Bruce, Nancy wondered if she should just invite the entire town, and then laughed to herself, because it was true that the entire town would be interested. After all, everyone knew Judith. You couldn't miss the flaming red-haired goddess who walked down the street talking to herself.

Taking out a slip of paper, she wrote herself a list of supplies to pick up. Judith would have plenty of things at the house to entertain, but she wasn't expecting such an enormous group. Besides, she wanted to pick up a banner that said "Congratulations" and get someone to hang it for her.

At the end of the afternoon, while Judith was finishing up with her last client, Nancy slipped out to go to the store. She left a note for Judith telling her where she went and that everyone would be at her house at 5:00.

What she neglected to tell her, or chose not to tell her, was how many people were coming. So when Judith pulled up at her house, thinking she would only see the Ruby Sisters and instead saw her house filled with people and a gigantic sign on the front door that said "Congratulations," she almost turned around and went the other way.

How could she have thought that the quiet decision that she and Bruce had made the night before would not turn into this kind of excitement? For them, it was a natural outcome of many discussions about who they were.

The hardest part for her was deciding to share her sexual history with Bruce, which was basically hardly any history at all. She shared why she had stayed away from dating relationships. They always revolved around the need for sex, and she explained to Bruce that she didn't have that need. That fact was not something she had ever shared with anyone.

She told him she kept that secret about herself because the world revolved around the drive to have sex and since she didn't have that drive, she didn't fit in. For a long time, she thought she was flawed. She didn't think that anymore, but she believed that because of who she was, it would not be possible to be in a relationship. She could never give another person what they wanted and deserved.

When Bruce had never pressured her that way, she was relieved at first. But when time went on, and she realized she loved him, she worried. Why hadn't he pressured her to have sex? Perhaps he didn't love her?

That night, it had all spilled out of her. When she finished telling him, Bruce had simply stared at her, and then wrapped her in his arms. She had thought for sure that she had ruined their relationship, and he was simply comforting her before saying goodbye.

But then he told her his secret. He too was asexual. Hours passed as they discussed what that meant. It didn't mean they didn't love intimacy. It didn't mean that they couldn't have sex together if they chose to. It didn't mean they wouldn't enjoy it. But it meant that they did not build their relationship on it, and with it or without it, they were together.

That night was when the two of them cemented their relationship together. After that, they knew that they had found everything they wanted by being with each other.

Last night had simply been the outcome of all that they had been sharing with each other. Bruce had rolled over in bed and held her hands and said, "If we make this official, you'll make me the happiest man in the world."

And she had said yes. Now it was time to face all their friends and let them gush over them. Judith hadn't realized she was still sitting in her car until Bruce knocked on her window.

"Shall we?" he asked, opening the door for her and helping her out of the car.

First she gave him a long kiss, knowing everyone was watching from the window, and said yes, just as she had said the night before.

Forty-Three

Cindy got Nancy's call while sitting on Emily's breathtaking dance deck. This enchanting spot had to be one of the most stunning places she had ever visited. The wooden deck cantilevered from the mountainside, creating a sensation of soaring through the air. Transparent glass partitions ensured the safety of the dancers, while leaving the spectacular view unobstructed.

Cindy couldn't imagine how glorious it must feel to dance on the deck, to paint pictures with movement and music. It was the first time she had wished she knew how to dance. Maybe she'd take Marsha up on her beginning adult dance class. That's if her life didn't explode in the meantime.

Leaning back, she watched the clouds float by and pretended she was riding them. Gigantic trees, both evergreen and deciduous, grew on the side and back of the deck. But the deck itself was open to the sky. Above them, hawks rode the currents, their wings spread open with a deep blue sky as the backdrop.

A beautiful meadow dotted with the white and yellow of Queen's Anne's lace and mustard plants spread out in front of the deck, leaving the view towards Doveland open.

Below the meadow, trees formed a canopy of green, with dots of yellow and red where some trees had begun to change colors. Cindy knew that no matter how wonderful an artist she was or wasn't, she would never come close to the artistry of nature.

From the deck, parts of the town were visible. The roads that led out from the center of the town's traffic circle headed off in all four directions. To the east, Cindy glimpsed the glimmer of a lake. Emily said to the west was Ava's house, and the bike and walking trail they could barely see through the trees were paid for by Ava and her husband Evan and built by her uncle's construction crew and teenagers he was mentoring.

Last night, after dinner, Emily had invited Cindy to come visit her retreat on the mountain on her way home. Cindy had hesitated at first, but Emily said she could show her the cottage where she could teach art next summer, and Grace had encouraged her to go.

Cindy didn't know what she expected, but what Emily showed her was far more beautiful than she could have imagined.

Every building looked as if it had sprouted from the mountain itself. There was Emily's home that she shared with her husband Josh, who taught writing. There was a dance studio, a place for the instructors to live, and, of course, an art cottage filled with light. Trees surrounded everything.

As they sat on the deck, Emily pointed out the large stone she used to sit on in the wildflower meadow as she dreamed about what she could build there.

When Cindy asked Emily how she ended up in Doveland and on this mountain, Emily told her it was a long story, but one she'd share with her when they had more time, which of course they would have if she came to teach.

The night before had been all about Cindy and her worries, so she had only heard bits and pieces of the stories Grace's group of women had to share. So she responded she would love to hear more about Emily and all the other women.

"So you'll come?" Emily had asked. "We have enough stories to share that we could entertain you all summer."

Cindy didn't answer at first. She could hear birds singing in the woods, some songs she recognized, others she didn't, and thought about how she felt about being away from the gallery and Spring Falls for a month or more. It would be a quiet adventure, and not that far from home. But she was worried.

"You still want me to come even though I explained I am not a talented artist?"

"Yes," Emily had replied. She didn't add that she was sure that Cindy was wrong about her artistic ability. And since Grace had shared with her some of what was going on in Spring Falls, she also knew that when Cindy returned, they would question her about Cedric's death. But there was no way she would believe that Cindy had killed anyone.

"Okay," Cindy said, and actually felt a glimmer of hope.

After explaining the entire story of her failed artist career and her summer at Cedric's to Grace's friends the night before, today some of the deep panic and humiliation was gone. Not all of it, though, and she was stalling about returning to Spring Falls because she wasn't at all sure she could handle the mess.

When Cindy's phone rang, interrupting the peace of the mountain, she glanced at the number, saw that it was Judith's office and had a moment of panic, thinking that maybe something terrible had happened.

She had the fleeting thought that it would be wonderful to stay right here on Emily's mountain and hide from everything that was going on in her life. She wanted to do that now, because next summer seemed a million years away.

However, when Nancy explained why she had called, Cindy's whole body lit up, and she monetarily forgot all about why she had run and what she was worried about.

"I'll be there," she said and stood up, her joints popping as she stretched a little.

"Time to go?" Emily asked.

Cindy explained that her best friend had just gotten engaged and there was going to be a little party for her in a few hours and she needed to be there.

As they walked up the mountain to her car, they both turned in time to see a hawk swoop down into the meadow and then fly away with something between its claws.

Cindy wondered if that was a sign of what was going to happen to her.

"Or you could be the hawk," Emily said, reading Cindy's thoughts.

Cindy pondered Emily's words as she drove home. Could she be like the hawk and capture the terror and secrets that had been feeding her artistic life all this time, and destroy them? Could she be free like the hawk?

But what about Daniel? Cindy asked herself. Does he care if I am not a great artist?

Will it surprise him to learn that she had been in New York when Cedric died? Would he believe that she did nothing, that she was too much of a coward to confront the art teacher who had destroyed her faith in herself?

Would anyone believe her? It was time to find out.

Forty-Four

Daniel was thankful he had taken the yoga class that morning, because if he hadn't, he was sure that the energy he felt bouncing off of him would be triple what it was right now.

It had been a good morning. Emily and her mother had gone with him for coffee after class, and he got to know a little more about the two of them. Not as much as he would have liked.

He thought Veronica was even more private about her life than he was. He had learned from Emma that her grandmother, Veronica's mother, had died when Veronica was Emma's age and that her grandmother had been an artist too.

While they were having coffee, Emma mentioned that she and her mother had moved a great deal, and after sharing some places they had lived, said that she liked Spring Falls best.

When he asked Veronica if the fact that her mother had died and she had lived with foster parents was the reason they moved around so much, Veronica had given Emma a look that meant she was probably in trouble for sharing that bit of information, and replied that maybe that was why, but mostly it was because she was restless.

He wondered how Veronica made a living that way, moving so much, but when he saw Veronica's bristle at his first question he kept that question to himself.

After coffee, Veronica and Emma went home, and he had run to the woods, sat on the bench and listened to the falls, trying to recreate the peace he had felt in yoga that morning.

Daniel's thoughts kept going to Cindy, his father, and how the universe had brought him to Spring Falls. Was it just to clear Cindy's name, assure her she was already the artist she wanted to be? Or was there more to the story?

Closing his eyes, he listened to the birds, felt the light breeze, and smelled the moist earth from the rain the night before. He finally achieved a small amount of relaxation when Steven texted him he was in town and was hungry.

Daniel suggested ParaTi's forgetting that was where Veronica worked. When Veronica teasingly asked if he was following her, he had laughed and introduced her to Steven.

Veronica had smiled, shook Steven's hand, and then apologized that she had to switch tables with someone else, so she couldn't be their server. During lunch Steven watched Veronica, and when Daniel asked why he was staring, he replied she seemed familiar.

"I had the same reaction too," Daniel said.

Steven took one last look, shrugged, and said, "Let's talk about this Cindy Jones. You think she's the one who painted the pictures stored in your father's studio?"

"I do. I don't know how those pictures got there, but the brief look I got at Cindy's paintings they were the same. More mature, even more beautiful, but obviously hers. She couldn't have come to the studio in New York and stolen his paintings, so it has to be the other way around."

"You know they are going to question her about your father's murder. She was in New York at the same time he died."

"They can question her all they want to, but it won't be true." Daniel paused before continuing. "One other thing. When I first met her, she seemed familiar. Yesterday I remembered why. She was a student of my father's. A long time ago. That's when I think he got her paintings."

Steven took another bite of his lunch, glanced again at Veronica, and squinted. So familiar, but too young to be a student of Cedric's. He had stopped teaching, probably when she was still a teenager.

"Well, I guess we'll find out more tonight. Bruce said that of course she'd be at the gathering at that woman Judith's house."

Daniel had laughed at the description. Judith was definitely someone you'd call 'that woman.' She was formidable.

And now, at Judith's house, where everyone was eating pizza, laughing and celebrating, all his efforts to relax were not working. He was too worried to be celebrating anything. Cindy hadn't arrived yet. And a storm was coming. They expected gusts of up to seventy miles an hour.

Safe in a house, that kind of wind might not be much, but out driving in it was dangerous. The ground was soaked because it had rained every night since he had come to town. Everyone said that it was good to be getting so much rain this time of year, it would ensure a beautiful showing of fall leaves. But soaked ground and trees with high winds were a recipe for disaster.

What was making him more nervous was the lights kept flicking on and off. Everyone expected a power outage. But Bruce had assured him it wouldn't matter because Judith had a generator that would automatically come on if the power failed.

Daniel wanted to say that wasn't what he was worrying about. It was Cindy driving alone in this weather. And he was wondering why no one else seemed worried.

"She's almost here," April said, coming to stand beside him as he stared out the window.

"How do you know?"

April showed him her phone with the find-a-friend app on it, and he could see that Cindy's car was only a few miles away.

"We make sure that we all know where we all are all the time. Judith made us install these back when Bree's husband died and Cindy went to get her. It's come in handy. Especially when I went off driving on my own for a few months. We all feel safer this way."

"I see I have missed quite a few stories about all of you," Daniel replied.

"Yes, you have. We'll share them in time, but right now, it is all about Cindy."

At the same time that the power went out, and the generator kicked on, April said, "See, there she is."

Without thinking, Daniel rushed out the door just as Cindy turned off the car. He was standing by her door when she stepped out of the car. She didn't protest when he wrapped her in his arms.

They stood for a minute, and then as it began raining, he shielded her the best that he could from the wind as they ran to the door, as the rain turned to hail and a branch from a tree shattered on the road.

Forty-Five

Veronica closed the curtains even though it was still afternoon. She hated the drapes. They were old and dirty, with faded flowers that couldn't have ever been a good choice for curtains. In fact, she hated everything about the apartment.

No matter how much she cleaned the floors or washed the windows, it felt like a prison cell. But it was what she could afford, and it was near everything which saved gas.

She wondered what it would be like to have a place of their own that opened to a garden. It was stupid to even think about such things because it could never happen.

She knew Emma hated the apartment too, but kept it to herself most of the time because she didn't want that to be the reason they moved again. When Daniel had asked why they always moved, she realized she had never answered that question for herself. Was she just restless? Or was it because she never knew her father and her mother died?

Was she unconsciously looking for a place to call home and nothing felt right? Maybe moving all the time was the same thing as wanting to go back to bed and pull the covers over her head.

But Emma was clear that Spring Falls felt right to her. That meant she would have to feel right to her too, because more than anything, she wanted Emma to be happy. Emma, her treasure. Emma who knew nothing about who she was, and she had hoped to keep it that way.

But now it might have become impossible, unless she moved again. Maybe that was why they always moved. She was running away from what she was, not towards a home.

It was good that Emma was in her bedroom, headphones on, listening to music, because she needed to think. She assumed Emma was listening to One Dimension given that appeared to be her favorite band at the moment,

Closing the curtains helped conceal the ugliness of the apartment, but did nothing to calm her fear. Maybe going back to bed and pulling the covers over her head would work. It had worked in the past.

At least she was home and not at work, where it was hard to conceal how she felt. The boss had closed ParaTi's for the evening because of the coming storm. He had said that it was too dangerous, adding that the electricity would probably go out, and then what would they do?

Everyone had gratefully agreed. They sent notices out to patrons who had reservations. Then the staff made sure the restaurant was clean and secure before leaving. There were shutters she had never noticed before by the side of each of the windows, and they were closed and latched. She learned that a small generator would kick on to keep the refrigerator and freezer running if the power went out.

On the way home, the wind had really started to blow and Veronica was glad they lived only a few blocks away. Although it was still fairly warm outside, the wind was cold and bitter and she had clutched her coat around her to keep warm. She found a wool stocking hat in a pocket, left over from last winter, and pulled it over her head.

Leaves and pieces of bark blew past her, as she rushed home, glad that Emma was safe and that she had stocked up on candles and lights just in case the power went out.

After pulling the curtains shut, despite the urge to retreat to her bed, she sat down in the one comfortable chair in the room. She decided to not notice how ugly the chair was, wrapped a blanket around her and tried not to think. *Deep breaths*, she told herself. And that had worked for an hour because she fell asleep. Working two shifts at ParaTi's was exhausting. But it was something she had to do. They needed the money.

When Veronica woke, she stayed in the chair, listened to the wind howling and tried to decide what to do. She wasn't sure how she had missed all the signs. Was she too self-absorbed? Too tired? Too worried? Probably all of those.

She had met Daniel with Emma. But never heard, or he never said, his last name. She was simply grateful that Emma, having met him, seemed more at peace with herself.

It wasn't until Daniel introduced her to Steven as an art dealer that she put the pieces together, and now that she had, she didn't know what to do. Run? She was tired of running. Tell Emma? She was just getting back into Emma's good graces. Telling her now might ruin everything.

Steven had kept staring at her at lunch, as if he was trying to place who she was. He didn't know her. She didn't know him. But when Daniel said he was an art dealer from New York, she had almost fainted. Panicked. Said she couldn't wait on their table. Had begged another waitress to take the table for her.

Because when Daniel said Steven was an art dealer, she knew who he was. Steven Binot had been Cedric's art dealer. And now she realized Daniel was Cedric's son. How she had missed that vital piece of information, she didn't know. She was an idiot.

And when Steven kept staring at her, she realized she must look familiar to him. Not because he knew her, but because he had probably met her mother. Eventually, he was going to put it all together.

What am I going to do? Veronica thought. Why did the universe bring me to this place? Was it to mock me? Make me face all of this? I barely knew Cedric. In fact, I didn't know him at all. But he knew me, and that's the problem.

Once everyone works this out, they'll know that I was also in New York when Cedric died. *It's going to be ugly no matter what,* Veronica thought. *Maybe we should run after all.*

But the wind howling outside made that impossible. If she kept her mouth shut, perhaps no one would discover who she was.

What amazed Veronica was that even as she had that thought, at the same time, she hoped someone would figure it out. Because perhaps then, she'd learn the entire story about who her mother was, and Emma would have a family.

As the wind slammed bits of bark and hail against the window, Veronica decided. She would take her life in her own hands. Tell what she knew. Stop running, and face the consequences. She hoped Emma would forgive her.

Forty-Six

As Daniel wrapped his arm protectively around her, guiding her out of the fierce wind and rain and into Judith's welcoming home, Cindy felt a sense of security. The world seemed to be spiraling into chaos, but when she was with Daniel, it felt as if none of that mattered—as if they could weather any storm together.

She had no time to process that realization before the door opened and she was pulled into the gathering. Everyone yelled, "Yay, it's Cindy," before surrounding her with hugs. In the process, she was separated from Daniel and discovered that without Daniel beside her, she felt bereft.

This is ridiculous, Cindy thought. *I barely know him.*

She glimpsed Daniel standing in the corner watching, and that made her feel better. And when he noticed her looking for him, he smiled and Cindy relaxed. He would not leave. He would not hold it against her that her paintings were terrible. So she relaxed and hugged people back, happy to be home.

Doveland was lovely. Emily's mountain was beautiful, but Spring Falls was her home. Who cared if she wasn't an artist? She had everything she ever wanted and needed in Spring Falls, and now there was the small possibility that she found someone who seemed to care about her. That was a miracle in itself.

Although Judith's generator was running, she had turned out all unnecessary lights, lit real candles on the coffee table, and placed fake ones in dark corners, making the entire house feel magical. They had all congregated in the living room, bringing their pizza and drinks with them.

Marsha scanned the room as everyone chatted and ate, noticing how everyone had paired off. She missed Nicky. After they resolved the Cindy thing, she'd have Nicky come to visit and stay for a while. Besides, they still hadn't had their grand opening at the Ruby House. Perhaps it was time for that to happen.

Marsha smiled to herself when she noticed even Nancy was paired off. At least she appeared to be thoroughly enjoying herself with Steven. He was much too old for her, but then Marsha was fairly sure Steven was gay, but that made it even better. Nancy and Steven could be friends and not worry about what else might have to happen.

Robert was sitting with his mother, and April looked years younger. Marsha knew that was because she was no longer worried that her children would be forever mad at her because of Ron. She had overheard the two of them talking about taking a trip to see her daughter and her family. Marsha hoped that happened, even though she'd miss her at the Ruby House.

Seeing Bree leaning back in Booker's arms made Marsha so happy she felt tears in her eyes. Addie had come with Booker. He didn't want to leave her in his house alone during the storm, and Addie was lying across Bree's lap and Bree didn't seem to mind. In fact, Bree looked downright blissful.

Mimi saw Marsha scanning the room, and Marsha smiled back at her. Marsha felt that Mimi and Janet had become a source of inspiration and comfort for her. They had been married for years, and survived the scrutiny and sometimes hate of people who didn't understand that who you loved wasn't a matter of what sex you were.

Marsha thought about how much she had learned from the two of them. Mimi and Janet were opposites, but with a single focus. "One heart," Mimi had once told Marsha about their relationship.

Despite it being a party to congratulate them on the engagement, Judith and Bruce were playing host and hostess. They were taking care of everyone, as they always did.

And then, of course, there were the two people—well maybe three, if you counted Steven—who were in the middle of a drama that could—no would—be the end of one life and the beginning of another for at least one of them. The question was whether that life would be a dream come true, or the beginning of a nightmare.

Cindy and Daniel were sitting together, not touching. Not yet sure what they were or could be. Marsha smiled at the two of them. She knew how that felt. Actually, they all knew how that felt. The last year had been a series of reveals, both good and bad. Reveals that changed everything.

But it brought us all together, Marsha thought. And we not only survived, we have thrived. She hoped that was what was going to happen to Cindy, too. Or maybe their luck had run out, and Cindy would pay the price.

For the next hour, the group shared stories, carefully avoiding the topic that concerned Cindy, but still giving Daniel and Steven a sense of the experiences they had all been through. Steven found himself amazed by what he heard. It reminded him of the seventies, when he was part of a community that shared in a similar manner, but this time without the drugs and alcohol.

Steven hadn't realized how much he missed having this kind of community. The art world was a cutthroat business, and in all the years he had been in it, he had ended up with just a few friends.

The friends from the old days were almost all gone now. He actually hadn't realized how old he was until now. Perhaps after settling the issue about the paintings, he'd retire and find some place warm to settle in and make friends before it was too late.

Judith checked the weather app on her phone and saw that the storm would persist until early morning. She announced to the group that it seemed they would need to have a sleepover, as driving in such high winds was far too dangerous. There was a significant risk of trees dropping limbs or toppling over.

Everyone mock-groaned. Except Daniel, Robert, and Steven, who looked stunned. A sleep over? How would that work?

Judith assigned her guest rooms to the couples. She said her office was for the extra women. They could decide who had the bed, and who would sleep on the cots that Bruce had retrieved from the basement.

That left Daniel, Robert, and Steven. The two sofas in the living room pulled out into beds, and with one cot they could decide who slept where.

By nine, everyone was settled into bed. Judith had enough bedding to take care of all the beds and cots. They left lights on in the kitchen so anyone who wanted to stay up could. Surprisingly, no one did.

The men in the living room discovered what young girls and women had known forever—that sometimes it was easier to talk in the dark, in a strange place. But what everyone avoided, on purpose, was why Steven was in town and what it could mean for Cindy and Daniel.

Robert couldn't help himself. As he felt sleep coming over him, he said, "Good night, John Boy," and the two men answered, "Good night Jim Bob, good night everyone."

Yep, Steven thought, *the seventies. Those were the days.*

Forty-Seven

Cindy woke in the middle of the night, listened for the sounds of the wind, and, not hearing anything, decided to get up. Everyone else was still sound asleep, but since she had slept in her clothes, she simply reached for her shoes and tiptoed out of the room. But not before gathering all the bedding from her cot and taking it to the laundry room. Just because she was leaving didn't mean Judith had to clean up after her.

Cindy stealthily made her way into the kitchen, aiming to avoid the living room where the men were sleeping. She slipped out the back door, knowing that Judith had disabled all the alarms during the windstorm. The swaying tree branches had been constantly triggering them, so she wasn't concerned about accidentally setting them off.

Taking a minute to look up at the now clear sky and the pinpoints of stars above her, Cindy breathed in the cool air and let herself feel as if she was part of the bigger universe. That feeling and awareness inspired her art, and she knew she would need all the reinforcement of something bigger than herself at work to get through the day.

It took longer to get home than usual. The street lights were out most of the way, but the moon showed her streets littered with tree limbs. One street was blocked off entirely by a large tree that had tipped over, its roots sticking out like a big brush. A crew was already there with chain saws and directed her down another street. She knew it would take days to clean up the fallen trees and repair the electric lines.

All the way home, while dodging tree limbs, she was wondering what to do about the paintings. Now that April and Daniel had seen them, was there any point in hiding them anymore? Or in keeping them?

Daniel had introduced her to Steven, but she never got a chance to ask Daniel why Steven was in town. She assumed it was because he and Daniel had to decide what to do with the rest of Cedric's paintings.

As she made a cup of coffee, Cindy was grateful that Judith had convinced her to get a generator that came on automatically. "Expensive, but worth it," was what Judith had said. And of course she was right because she had a warm house and coffee even though the power was still out.

She hadn't gotten around to getting a generator for the art gallery. She'd have to add it to things for Seth to do before he finished with the upstairs renovations.

With her coffee in hand, Cindy trudged upstairs to her studio, and not bothering to turn on the light, lowered herself into the only chair in the room. There were many times that she had given up painting for the day and sunk into the chair and fallen asleep.

Not this time. This time, she was wide awake. The moon light shone in through the skylights, illuminating the stack of paintings facing the wall. She was looking at all her failures. Years of work for nothing.

The painting on the easel was the only one visible, revealing to April and Daniel that she had been painting all along, but was not an artist.

Or that was what she thought had happened. Now she understood. Alone in the moonlight, she had to admit that it was possible she had it all wrong. Daniel, April, and Robert said they loved the paintings. That's what they were trying to tell her when they saw her at the gallery. But she was so sure that what Cedric had told her was real, she hadn't heard them. She had run away instead.

But now she was ready to listen, even though acknowledging what they said only brought fresh pain. She had hid her paintings away all these years because she had believed a lie? What kind of fool was she? And then there was Daniel. He was Cedric's son. She liked him, and she knew he liked her. Despite that, he was Cedric's son.

Did he know what a horrible man his father was? What would he say if he knew his father had seduced her that summer? She was just a girl, really. Young, naïve, barely understanding how the world worked. That summer had forced her to grow up. But had she really? Cedric's charm and assurance about who she was and what she would never be had wormed its way into her life and kept her believing that what he told her was true.

His declaration of love for her certainly wasn't true. Well, she never believed that anyway. It was only a matter of egos that put her into that relationship. His and hers. Hers because she wanted to be important to him. Did she care that he was married and had a son? No. She was young and stupid, but not so stupid as to fall for his promise that he would always care for her.

But now she realized she had fallen for his other lie. That she wasn't ever going to be a great artist. He told her that her work was mundane. Just decoration.

And because she believed him, she decided that there was no reason to take home the work she had done while she was with him that summer. In a fit of pique, she had stormed out one day and left them there, and told no one.

For years, she had lived with this secret. It was only last week that she decided to just teach art and stop trying to be an artist herself.

And then Daniel came to town, and it was as if a puzzle piece had snapped into place. Everything about him felt right. Yes, he was ten years younger. But he didn't care, so she didn't care either.

Yes, it had been only a few days since she met him, but all her friends believed in love at first sight, couldn't she? But he was Cedric's son. Cedric, the root of all her worst secrets.

Why hadn't Daniel said his last name when she first met him? But even if he had, would she had known then? Jacobs was a popular name. Why would she associate him with Cedric? She had only realized who he was when Judith introduced Steven to the room as Cedric's art dealer. She had hidden her shock from everyone, even though it felt as if ants had buried themselves in her skin, making her want to scream.

Discovering the truth about Daniel was just like the windstorm. It blew down everything she thought she had in place. All evening, sitting beside Daniel on the couch, she had tried not to react. And then she went off to bed, saying nothing to anyone, keeping all her fears and worries locked up inside her.

But now she had time to think and prepare for what was coming. Everything was going to come out into the open. What would Daniel think when he learned about her affair with his father? Would he hate her or be disgusted? Would he believe she killed Cedric?

Tears streamed down Cindy's face, making silver streaks in the moonlight. But there was no one there to see them. Until that moment, Cindy hadn't fully accepted how lonely she was—how much of her life had been locked up in that room. If paintings could talk, they would tell her she was a fool and always had been.

Today was the day all her secrets were going to be revealed. Her visit to see Cedric. Her history with him. Her paintings.

The rest of her life depended on if they believed what she told them. But how could she expect them to? Because at this point, she wasn't even sure if she knew what was real and what wasn't.

Forty-EIght

Judith slipped out of bed and into the kitchen, trying not to wake anyone. But she found Daniel and Steven already in the kitchen drinking coffee. Taking cinnamon buns out of the freezer, she put a few on a plate and popped them into the microwave.

As the food warmed up, Bruce, Bree, and Booker joined the group, prompting Judith to decide on preparing breakfast for everyone. She scrambled all the eggs in the refrigerator and defrosted all the cinnamon buns from the freezer. One by one, the rest of the group made their way into the kitchen.

When April and Marsha told the group that Cindy was not in the house, there was a moment of stillness while everyone worried about why she had left. But checking their phones and seeing that she was at home, they knew she was safe, and not running away again.

"She probably just needs to think things through," Judith said, and everyone nodded in agreement.

After giving it some thought, Booker decided it would be better to visit Cindy at her house for their conversation. The new police station was often filled with construction noise, and he believed

Cindy would feel more comfortable talking in her own home. So, following breakfast, he dropped Bree off at her place and then headed to Cindy's house.

As he drove, he prayed Cindy had a reason for being in New York and an alibi for the time Cedric was killed. The last thing he wanted was to arrest the woman who had rescued Bree when she was drowning in grief over her husband's death.

Booker wasn't glad that Paul had died, but he was grateful that Paul's last gift to Bree had reunited the Ruby Sisters and had brought Bree back to Spring Falls. To him.

As always, when Booker thought of Paul, he thanked him for what he had done. He knew Paul couldn't hear him, but maybe wherever he was, he could feel his gratitude. Booker didn't expect Bree to ever stop loving Paul, but he knew she loved him too, and that was more than enough for him.

Pulling up to Cindy's house, he sighed, wishing he didn't have to be there for this reason. But it was a good thing he was the one questioning her. Unlike some of his colleagues, he would listen and not make assumptions.

Cindy's normally neat front yard was littered with small twigs and tree limbs. He knew she had a service that cleaned up her yard for her, although he doubted they would make it to her house today. The whole town was going to be a mess for a while.

Across the street from Cindy, a gigantic pine tree had fallen. It was obvious why. It was completely hollow inside. Booker wondered how it had stood for so long like that before the wind pushed it over.

Cindy was sitting by the window in the living room, and she waved at him to come in. Booker wondered if she was watching for him, or hoping for someone else. Her face when he opened the door told him it wasn't him she was watching for.

"I'm sorry, Cindy," he said, as she let him in. He had dropped Bree at home, but he still had Addie with him. He hoped that

Addie's presence would help Cindy feel more relaxed, and as she bent to hug her, he knew he had made the right decision.

"You've come to interrogate me, haven't you?" Cindy said, straightening to look up at him. Last night, Judith had filled her in on what was happening around Cedric's death. So she was ready.

"Not interrogate, Cindy. Just get clarification. If we need to, we will go down to the station, but right now, this is just a friendly interview."

"Will Daniel need to know what we talk about today?"

"What do you think, Cindy? How much do you like him? Could you keep whatever your secret is from him and still be happy?"

Cindy led Booker into the living room, saying nothing, but once she sat down, she shook her head.

"You're right. I couldn't. What do you think about letting him hear the story as I tell it to you? It will be easier for me to tell it once."

Booker nodded and made a phone call.

"He'll be here in a few minutes. In the meantime, could you show me the paintings everyone is raving about?"

"No one is raving about them," Cindy said, trying to conceal the tiny sliver of hope that had flared in her heart.

"Oh, but they are. April, Robert, and of course Daniel, said they were stunning. It's why Steven is in town, you know."

"No, it isn't. He's here to talk to Daniel about selling his father's paintings."

Booker studied Cindy and realized she still didn't understand. But then, how could she? She had been living with a lie for years. It was a hollow lie, like the trunk of the tree across the street. And like that tree, the life she had built around that lie had toppled over.

"Let's talk about that when Daniel gets here. In the meantime, may I see the paintings?"

Putting her coffee down, Cindy led the way upstairs to her studio. She had never willingly let someone in to see her work. She had waited years, hoping one day she would turn out a piece of art that would move people, and she could call herself an artist.

And now, finally, she was showing them to a police officer who could arrest her at any moment. That was terrifying, but what was even more terrifying was what he would say when he saw her art.

Cindy, who had lived most of her life in the desperate wish that she was an artist and a deeply entrenched belief that she wasn't, held her breath as she opened the door, stood back, and let Booker into the room.

When he stood in front of the painting on the easel without a word, her heart broke, and then she saw his face and realized she had gotten it all wrong before. She could blame it on Cedric, but really, she could have chosen not to believe him.

Now, the question was, was it too late for it to matter? Or had she ruined her chances by going to New York to see Cedric?

For the moment, though, she let herself feel the joy that had started to beat out of her heart and into every pore of her body. Standing in the doorway of her studio, Cindy smiled at Booker and he smiled back, making everything perfect, at least for the moment.

Forty-Nine

The sun streaming through the curtains woke Emma. She lay still, listening, and could only hear the hum of the small refrigerator in their room. The horrible wailing noise of the wind during the night had been terrifying. So much so she had wanted to go to her mother's bed and crawl in like she did when she was a little girl.

But she wasn't little anymore, so instead, she had pulled the covers over her head and tried not to hear the howling, grateful that they were warm and safe.

Yesterday, her mother had done something completely unexpected, and it had so delighted Emma she still couldn't believe it had happened. Her mother had come home from work explaining that ParaTi's was closed because of the coming storm, and declared that they were going some place else to wait out the storm.

"The electricity will probably go out, and this place isn't safe. Or warm. So let's go!"

Emma had stared at her mother as if she had never seen her before, and thought that she might not have. Might never have fully looked at the person standing in front of her. Not as a mother, but as a person.

"Yes!" was all she could say at the moment, but she knew her mother understood how happy she was to not be stuck in the scary apartment. They had found a pretty motel just outside of town, been assured that there was a generator that would kick on if the electricity went off, and settled in for the night.

For both of them, it was a moment of declaration. No more living in terrible places, no more fighting between the two of them. Although the wind was frightening, it was the best time they had together in months and months. They watched a few TV shows, some they liked, some they didn't, played cards, and finally settled in for the night, trying not to hear the screeching wind.

Before climbing into bed, Emma had looked out the window to see the whole town was dark. If it hadn't been so terrifying outside, she would have loved to have gone out into the parking lot to look at all the stars without all the ambient light that kept most of them hidden.

She had heard about places that didn't have light that blocked out the stars and someday she was going to visit them all and paint what she saw. She could never create paintings like Van Gogh's Starry Starry Night, but she could paint her view of how the world looked.

This morning, now that the storm had passed, it felt like a brand new day with a newly happy mother, and she wanted food. Rolling over, she saw her mother still in bed buried in blankets, reading a book. Taking a leap from her bed, Emma bounced onto her mother's bed, making them both laugh.

"Let's go see if the coffee shop has electricity. If it does we can get coffee and food, and then head over to the art gallery? I want to find out how soon the art school will open," Emma said as soon as they stopped laughing.

Veronica smiled at her daughter, feeling happier than she had for months, and said, "Yes, let's!"

• • • ● • ● • • •

They ended up having breakfast in the motel's diner, not sure if there was power in town. Emma had pecan waffles and her mother had a stack of pancakes. Not their usual morning breakfast, once again making the statement that they were starting a new phase of their life together.

But when they got to town, they saw the coffee shop was open and Emma talked her mother into buying coffee for Mimi and Janet, hoping that they would be at the gallery to receive them.

Not that she was sucking up to them (or maybe she was) but she thought they were two of the coolest women she had ever met, and she wanted to let them know that. Maybe coffee would help?

She hadn't really needed to talk her mother into it. She had smiled and said, "That's a good idea!" Emma didn't know what had gotten into her mother, but she loved it.

And when Veronica had put her arm around her as they waited for the coffee, and said, "Have I ever told you that you are my treasure?" Emma hadn't resisted the hug as she had in the past. She let herself be held and giggled as she answered, "Just a few times, mom."

Emma smiled up at her mother, remembering what her mother had told her about the note her grandmother had gotten from her best friend in art school. She wondered who that best friend had been, and if she was still around.

They walked to the art gallery, since it was just a few blocks down from the coffee shop, Veronica holding the coffees secure in the carrier, but when they got there, the art gallery door was locked. Emma knocked on the door, hoping someone would hear it. It was Janet who came out of the back room to see who was there. Seeing Emma, Janet did a little skip of delight and rushed to open the door.

Emma couldn't believe someone would be that happy to see her. But mostly she couldn't believe that someone could be so full of joy that they skipped in delight. *Does Janet see the entire world as a treasure,* she asked herself, and realized it was entirely possible.

Veronica held out the coffees, and Janet yelled for Mimi to come see who was there. Mimi didn't skip out of the office, but her face showed her delight at seeing the two of them.

"We came to see if we could help with anything," Veronica said.

Emma nodded, realizing that her mother liked these two women, too. Once again, she looked at her mother as a person and not just as her mother, and realized her mother had always been as lonely as Emma was. And now she wasn't.

Feeling as if her heart would burst open with happiness because now she knew for sure they wouldn't be leaving Spring Falls, she added, "And to find out when art classes start."

"Well, those are two fantastic reasons," Mimi said. "We could use some help, and most of that is up in the studio space. The sooner we get that done, the sooner the classes can begin."

It was only when Emma asked, "Is Cindy here?" that the mood darkened.

"What's happening?" Emma asked.

"It's nothing really," Mimi answered. "It's just that Cindy was in New York at the time that Daniel's father died, so they are questioning her to see if she knows anything."

"Who was Daniel's father?" Emma asked.

"An artist by the name of Cedric Jacobs."

Veronica was relieved that no one was looking at her. They were all busy looking at the studio when Mimi answered Emma's question.

As her world crumbled around her, Veronica's thoughts stayed on Emma.

This studio is perfect, she thought. *Emma will love it here.*

Although dirty from construction, the studio was filled with light. The windows on the inside wall looked down into the gallery, and the skylights framed the clear blue sky, all the clouds chased away by the wind.

But for Veronica, the storm had returned. She knew exactly who Cedric Jacobs was, and now she wished that she had never gone to New York to see him.

Fifty

Daniel arrived while Booker and Cindy were still in her studio. When the doorbell rang, Cindy nodded and Booker yelled, "Come in, we're upstairs."

For Cindy, having two people in her private studio to look at her painting was surreal and more than a little unsettling. She had kept this part of her life separate for so long that it felt as if they were invading her privacy. She had to resist the voice in her head that made her want to scream at them to get out.

No, she said to herself. *I want them both here. I want to hear the truth, and I am going to tell the truth. The whole truth?* The voice in her head demanded, and she answered, *Yes, the whole truth.*

Daniel shifted his gaze from the painting he adored to find Cindy standing in the studio's corner, nervously fiddling with the buttons of her yellow sweater. To him, she resembled a ray of sunlight momentarily obscured by a cloud, yet her inner light still shone through.

It's what he had seen as a boy so many years before. Cindy, her blond hair framed by the light in his father's studio and blue eyes so bright he could see their color across the room.

She hadn't been looking at him, though. She had been staring at his father. And now, looking back, he saw what that little boy didn't see. She had been in love with his father. Like all the women who came through the studio or met his father at one of his many art openings, they were putty in his hand. Until they got to know him.

Before his mother passed away, she had explained his father to him. She wanted him to know that he wasn't like his father at all. That Cedric was a world of his own. One that kept him as the star, a world he designed so he would always be the one in control. And eventually, everyone that knew him discovered the truth that his ego never let him care about anyone. If it served him, he did it. If it didn't, he walked away.

As Daniel watched Cindy now, he thought he knew what his father had done. He had destroyed her belief in herself. He told her she would never be an artist, and she had believed him.

That was why the paintings were in his father's studio. That was why these paintings faced the wall as if they were worthless. But for Daniel, the room was filled with treasure. Not just the paintings which he knew Steven would see as priceless, but the woman who had dropped her head, afraid to look at him.

Did she think she was too old for him? That he would care that his father had fooled her, and she had slept with him? Yes, he cared. But not the way she thought. If his father were in front of him now, he'd want to punch him. Not a reaction he had ever had with anyone.

Booker turned to see Daniel staring at Cindy, who refused to look at either of them, and said, "It's time to tell the story, Cindy."

Cindy nodded wordlessly, but as she moved to leave the room, Daniel put his hand on her arm and said, "These paintings are extraordinary, Cindy. I've never seen anything as lovely."

Booker nodded in agreement, adding, "I know nothing about art, but I love this painting," and smiled to himself because he knew Daniel also meant that he had never seen anything as lovely as Cindy.

He recognized the look in Daniel's eyes. It was the one he had when he saw Bree again after all the years they were apart. It was a yearning for the woman he loved to see how he felt and to acknowledge and return it.

As they headed downstairs, Cindy leading the way so neither of the two men could see the tears in her eyes, Booker hoped that whatever Cindy told them would prove without a doubt that she had not killed Cedric.

He knew she hadn't. All her friends knew she couldn't have done such a thing, but he needed proof to move the eyes of the law away from her and let her get on with her life.

They ended up sitting around the kitchen table, a cup of coffee in front of each of them, Cindy's untouched.

"Before you begin," Daniel said, "I want to tell you my part of this story, because I think it will help."

Booker nodded.

"I saw you years ago in my father's studio, Cindy. I know you are going to tell us that my father seduced you, because that is what he did.

"He was a horrible man, and a mediocre artist who convinced others he was a great artist. And one way he did that, I know now, was to copy your style. That's what made him famous.

"His painting changed dramatically after your summer with him. It made him rich. And Cindy, I know all that because I saw the paintings you left there, so we can prove what I am saying.

"But most of all, I want you to know, Cindy, that I don't care what happened that summer. And neither should you."

Cindy stared at Daniel for a long moment before asking, "You saw me that summer? I don't remember."

Cindy knew that there was much more to what Daniel had said, but that he knew her for that long, and understood what had happened and didn't seem to care, was almost more than she could comprehend.

"I did. I was just a little boy of ten then, and you were a grown woman. You waved at me, but why would you remember? My father was like a giant force that filled every space. But I saw you, another woman, and two men."

Cindy breathed out, thinking about how extraordinary the world was.

"Linda. The other woman was Linda. I wonder what happened to her. The two men left earlier, leaving us with him. I think that was his intention. To make them leave him alone with us."

Booker listened to the story and thought that all of this made Cindy an even more likely suspect in Cedric's death.

Cindy realized that too, because she turned to Booker and said, "And now you really need to know why I was in New York, don't you? Now you know what he did to me. It's highly possible that I finally had enough and went there to confront him."

Booker nodded yes.

"And it's true. That's exactly what I went to New York to do. I was finally angry enough to want to see him and make him pay for ruining my dreams."

"And did you, Cindy? Make him pay for what he did?"

Before Cindy could answer, Booker's phone rang, and seeing that it was the station, answered it.

Daniel and Cindy watched his face change as he listened. Cindy was anxious to tell her story and get it over with, and Daniel was determined that no matter what she said, he'd stick by her.

"Let's go."

"Where?"

"To the station. There's been a development."

Cindy's heart sank. For a moment, she thought she'd be free. Now she was afraid she wouldn't be.

Fifty-One

Judith and Bruce stood in her kitchen looking at the stack of dishes and pans on the stove and laughed.

"I feel as if I just fed an army," Judith said.

"You did!" Bruce laughed.

April and Robert had collected all the bedding and were doing the laundry. Marsha and Nancy were remaking all the beds with clean sheets, leaving Judith and Bruce in the kitchen with Steven.

"Is it always like this around here?"

"Depends on what you mean by that," Judith answered.

Steven waved his hands around to take in the kitchen and all the activity going on in the house.

"I guess it is. Now. For years, it was just Cindy and me in Spring Falls. All the Ruby sisters had gone off on their own. April and Bree moved away with their husbands and Marsha went off to New York."

"I think I saw her once, in a Broadway play. It took a minute to place her, but when you introduced everyone, I was sure. She was quite extraordinary."

"She still is," Nancy said, having overheard the conversation as she returned to the kitchen. Nancy believed one of her most valuable gifts was the ability to overhear almost anything, or figure out what people were talking about by hearing just a few keywords.

She thought it was amazing how much she could piece together about what was happening just by listening and paying attention. It made her very good at her job and provided her with an extra bit of entertainment everywhere she went.

Judith knew almost everyone in town, and almost everyone knew her too. But Nancy was proud of the fact that she knew everyone, too. But not everyone knew her, and she liked it that way.

She had to admit to herself that she had hoped she'd hear Steven say something about her, but no such luck. Besides, it was embarrassing to be thinking about herself at that moment, when Cindy was having such a hard time.

"I agree," Judith said. "Every Ruby Sister is extraordinary, and that includes Nancy. My business runs as well as it does because of Nancy."

"Mine too," Bruce chimed in. "And speaking of business, I have an appointment with a client that I need to keep, so I'm off."

Judith knew Bruce had a client in hospice care and he couldn't, wouldn't, cancel.

"Me too," Nancy said. "Time to go manage that well run business of yours, Judith. Thanks for taking me in last night. That was an interesting way to celebrate your engagement! A wind storm and a sleepover. We'll be talking about that for a long time!"

Steven smiled at Nancy as she turned to leave, hoping he'd get to see her later, and when she smiled back, he thought maybe she was telling him it was up to him.

"So the town's power is back on?"

"Doesn't really matter. My office has a generator too."

Steven knew she meant a machine when she said generator, but what he thought was that Judith was the generator. She kept everyone running, and to him, it looked as if she did it all effortlessly.

Judith's phone beeped. It was Cindy with a simple text message. "I'm at the police station."

Nancy had just reached the front door, and Judith called out to her, "Cancel my appointments today, please."

Turning to Steven, she said, "Come with me. You might be able to help."

Although he had just met her, Steven knew enough not to argue with the red-haired woman. For a second, he thought he saw her red hair light up, but since that was impossible, put it down to a flash of sunlight.

"Where are we going?"

"First, we are going to Cindy's so you can see the paintings, and then we are going to the police station."

A few minutes later, Steven was standing in front of a painting in the same style as Cedric's, but so much more beautifully done it took his breath away. Judith turned around a few of the paintings that were leaning against the wall so that he could see them, too. They looked the same as the ones in Cedric's studio that Daniel hadn't let him sell yet. But these were better, as if the artist had matured and found her voice.

Sitting down in Cindy's chair, he dropped his head into his hands. "So Cindy is the artist? And Cedric copied her work all these years?"

"You tell me. You're the expert. That's what happened, isn't it?"

Steven didn't need to answer the question. The evidence was right in front of them. The trouble was, if Cindy had found out what Cedric had done, would the police think she would be angry enough to kill him? Steven didn't know.

But he was angry. Cedric had fooled him all these years. Well, not fooled, he must have known. But Steven knew he had ignored his gut feelings because Cedric's paintings had sold well. He had turned a blind eye to who Cedric had been, and never questioned how his work changed from one style to another. He thought Cedric had simply read the market and painted what sold.

Well, he had been right. Those paintings had sold. And now Cindy's paintings would, too. And the cynical art dealer in him knew they'd sell even better because of the scandal.

On the other hand, he wasn't sure Judith or her friends would let it get to that. It would be better all around if he supported what Judith intended to do. He had played around with a devil for too long. It was time to be on the side of the angels.

"That's enough," Judith said, as if she could read his mind. "Now, you are going to help my friend."

Fifty-Two

"We really have to stop meeting this way," Judith said, seeing the crowd of people in the new waiting room.

Since the entire police station had to be rebuilt following Ron Page's arson, they had taken the opportunity to modernize everything. The waiting room was now much more comfortable than before. While it still maintained a serious atmosphere befitting its purpose, it was a significant improvement over the previous room, which had only a few metal chairs for seating and not much else.

At least this one had beautiful wooden benches that April had rescued from an old church. April had asked if she could help with the redesigning of the building. Her husband had burnt it down, and she wanted to be part of building it up again.

In another room a circular saw whined and there were little dust particles floating in the air from the construction, but Booker had said the building was almost finished, and with the door closed to the inside of the station it wasn't too bad.

As Judith stood in the doorway, she remembered the last time she had been here. Last spring, she had come to confront Ginny about what she had done and to protect Bree and April.

Today she was on the same kind of mission. She was here to protect Cindy, because she knew it was impossible for Cindy to have been responsible for Cedric's death. But it bothered her she hadn't known that Cindy went to New York a few months ago. Why hadn't she told her?

After all, almost every Monday morning for years and years, they had coffee together. They told each other everything. Well, almost everything. Because Cindy had shared nothing about either her art or her trip. However, Judith knew Cindy was incapable of violence, so she trusted that there was a reasonable explanation.

The last time she had been at the police station, she had Nicky with her to help her unravel that mystery. This time, it was Steven. She hoped Steven could help as much as Nicky had with Ron Page.

However, there were two people sitting in the waiting room she never expected to see there: Veronica and Emma. So with Cindy, Booker, Daniel, Emma, Veronica, Steven, and her, it was a crowd.

Which is why she had said, "Let's stop meeting this way." She hoped it was the last time they met in a police station to rescue someone. But at least she knew Bree and Marsha were safely at home, and then they too walked into the station.

"What are you two doing here?"

"We can't just sit by and let Cindy be accused of something she didn't do."

At which point Cindy burst into tears. Within minutes, all the Ruby Sisters had surrounded her.

Booker looked around the waiting room and marveled at how quickly he had lost control. Maybe he could round them up and put them all in the small room where he met with his officers.

It would be better than the waiting room where other people would come in to complain about something relatively trivial, like their neighbor's trash can always ending up in their yard, or a local dog using their lawn as a toilet.

Booker knew he should interview each of them separately, but he doubted he'd get much cooperation that way. He had a feeling that it would be better to hear them all out together. Not a good police procedural, but then he didn't really believe that Cindy killed Cedric, either.

However, there was something else going on with Emma and her mother, Veronica. Maybe he should talk to them separately. Veronica took the decision about what to do first out of his hands when she stood up and said, "I have to confess something."

"Mom!" Emma said. "Stop it."

"No, honey, this has gone on long enough. I have to share a secret I have kept all my life. It's time for you to know who I am."

Booker stood in front of Veronica and quietly asked, "Are you sure you want to do this now? What does this have to do with Cedric's death?"

Veronica whispered to Booker, "I have to." Then turning to the group she said, "I knew Cedric too. Well, I didn't know him until recently. I met him a few months ago. In New York."

When Booker hesitated, she said, "Let me tell the whole story. To everyone. I'd rather get this over with all at once."

Emma had stepped back and stared at her mother. For the third time that day, she looked at her and saw her as a person and not just as her mother. This time, she was horrified. Her mother was going to tell a secret that was going to ruin her life. She was sure of it.

Never in a million years would she have thought that her mother knew the famous artist Cedric Jacobs. How? Did this have something to do with her grandmother being an artist?

Emma saw Daniel standing at the edge of the group, as if he was trying to disappear. He caught her eye and the two of them stared at each other. Emma thought he felt the same way. Confused and frightened. But why was he? What did he have to do with Cedric Jacobs?

Booker looked at the group, which was now closed in around Emma and Veronica, and sighed.

"Alright. This is not as it's supposed to be done, but let's do it. Tell your story to everyone. And then Cindy, it's your turn."

Judith texted Bree, "Get to the police station right now. You'll want to hear this."

And then whispered to Booker, "Waiting for Bree."

Booker looked at her as if she was crazy.

"We can't do this without Bree."

All Booker could think was, heaven help anyone who tried to hurt a Ruby Sister.

"Five minutes. Get everyone in the meeting room. I'll round up more chairs."

Seeing Judith's text, Bree hadn't stopped to think. She grabbed her purse and ran out the door and made it to the station as everyone was settling into the room. She smiled, seeing Booker at the front of the room, looking both stern and worried.

Booker took courage from Bree's smile, turned to face the room, and said, "Who is starting this?"

Veronica stood and said, "I will."

Cindy looked up at Veronica and finally realized why she looked so familiar.

"You look just like my friend."

"I do, don't I?"

Emma, who had just seen a picture of her grandmother and thought that her mother looked just like her, understood what the two of them meant.

"You knew my grandmother?"

"Yes, I did."

And then Cindy understood what Veronica was going to say and burst into tears again. Cedric had ruined Linda's life, too.

Fifty-Three

"Somebody explain to me what is happening," Steven asked.

In his entire life, Steven had never been with such a strange group of people. And he represented artists, for heaven's sake. Artists were strange in their own way. This group of people was entirely different. Maybe because it was a community, not a competition.

The only competition going on here was who was going to talk first about Cedric. Steven had the ridiculous thought that he wished Nancy was there too, not for any other reason than he couldn't wait to see her again, and he didn't want her to hear any of this second hand.

"Sit down!" Booker yelled from the front of the room. "I am going to ask the questions. You will all be quiet unless I am talking to you. If you have something to say, raise your hand."

Someone started giggling at the back of the room, and Booker glared at all of them. "I mean it! Otherwise, I will talk to you one at a time. In the interrogation room.

"Cindy, Veronica, Steven, and Daniel are the ones that this mess revolves around. Come to the front of the room. The rest of you sit still. I'm going to start the story as I know it. Then you to tell me the rest. Agreed?"

Everyone nodded, and Bree tried not to smile at Booker, expecting that might throw him off the stern guy approach. She noticed he was doing his best not to look at her.

Although there was still a tiny tittering in the back of the room, and he suspected it was Marsha, Booker pretended not to hear it.

Booker looked at Cindy, trying to ignore her tear-stained face, knowing that if he could get the facts of what happened, he might be able to relieve some of her stress. On the other hand, it could make it worse. But it was his job to find out. Better him than someone who didn't care.

"Cindy, I understand you studied with Cedric Jacobs years ago. Fill me in on what happened that summer."

Glancing at Veronica, who had her hand raised, Booker said, "Not yet."

"Wait, I think we should start with Veronica, if you don't mind," Cindy said, making her voice sound strong and sure. Now that she knew who Veronica was, she knew she had to protect her.

"Shouldn't we address the elephant in the room? Because, yes, I did go to study with Cedric. But so did Veronica's mother, Linda."

Even though everyone in the room had put the pieces together, hearing it said out loud silenced everyone. Veronica stared at Cindy, hungry to hear the story she had never heard. She reached out and held Emma's hand, hoping what they heard wouldn't ruin the life they were building.

Veronica prayed Emma would understand why she never told her the little of what she had known. Maybe if Emma understood why she kept it a secret, she would forgive her.

The question Veronica had always asked herself was if she was ashamed of her mother. At that moment, Veronica knew she wasn't. And she hoped Emma wouldn't be ashamed of her either.

Smiling at Veronica, Cindy continued, feeling a mix of relief and fear. What would her friends say? What would Daniel think? But she knew she didn't have a choice. She had to tell the complete story now that she had started.

"I had an affair with Cedric. I was twenty. So was Linda. We knew nothing about the world, or men. Especially men like Cedric. I know he was your father, Daniel, but I think you have accepted that he was a terrible person."

Daniel said nothing, just stared straight ahead, hoping if he didn't look at anyone, he wouldn't break apart. He knew who his father was, but hearing it from Cindy made him want to run out of the room. But he knew Cindy was telling the truth, and truth telling was important to him. Unlike his father.

Cindy took a deep breath, tried not to worry that Daniel wouldn't look at her, and continued. She didn't care that fresh tears had started or that her voice was cracking from the tension of telling this long-held secret.

"Somehow Cedric wound people around and around until they didn't know what they were doing. He would be emotionally abusive, then so kind your heart would melt. And then he'd do it again. The cycle. It worked. I forgot myself.

"And I suspected later that the same thing happened to Linda. Of course, we wouldn't have talked about it. Cedric was clear that it had to remain our secret, otherwise he would make sure we never worked in the art world.

"What did I know about that? I thought he had power, and I suppose he did. Because, for all these years, I have believed that what he told me was true. That I was a failure as an artist.

"I know he told that to Linda too. I tried to tell her she was a treasure, especially to me. But she got more and more depressed as the summer went on. I suppose I did too. Maybe I have been for all these years. But I know what happened to Linda was different."

Cindy turned to Veronica and, holding both her hands, her voice cracking, she said, "You are Linda's daughter, aren't you?"

When Veronica nodded, she added, "And Cedric Jone was your father."

Numbly, Veronica nodded again.

Cindy looked at Daniel, who had finally turned to look at her, his face white and his blue eyes darker than normal, and nodded.

While still holding Veronica's hands, she added, "Which means, of course, Daniel, that Veronica is your half-sister. And Emma is your niece."

Daniel thought he was ready to hear what he had suspected as he listened to Cindy explain that summer. And he had started his journey after his father's death to find siblings, assuming, hoping, that he had a few. Nevertheless, now that he knew, and it was real, he didn't know what to do.

But looking at Veronica and Emma, he realized he had already begun to love them both. This was going to be easy. It was a gift.

For a moment, the entire room was quiet and still, like the eye of a hurricane. Then it erupted as everyone tried to say something at once. No one was entirely sure if that news helped Cindy, or hurt her, but they were happy for Daniel, Veronica, and Emma, who were hugging so tightly they looked like one person. All three of them were tall and dark, looking enough like one another that Judith wondered how she hadn't noticed it before.

Although Booker tried to quiet the room, he gave up and let the noise continue, knowing the story wasn't done, and eventually, they would all want to know the rest of it.

As Daniel embraced Veronica and Emma, he whispered to them, "I am so happy to have found you."

Emma thought her heart would burst wide open. Daniel Jacobs was her uncle. The nicest man she had ever met. But then she realized she was also the granddaughter of a terrible man. And she still had to worry about why her mother was in New York to see him.

Booker let the room take in the news and as it became quieter, said, "Great. You can all do this family meeting thing later. Right now, we still don't know what Cindy and Veronica were doing in New York."

Turning to the two of them, who were now bookending Daniel, he added, "You both admit you went to see him. What happened when you did? Cindy you believed he had ruined your art career. And Veronica, you found out he was your father and were angry about it. So what did you two do? Did one of you kill him?"

Before either of them could protest, Steven stood, waited until everyone was looking at him, and said, "No, they didn't. I did."

Fifty-Four

"Sit," Booker yelled. He never yelled, and this was the second time he had done it in one morning.

The room quieted, but was not still. And he wanted still, but he knew it would not happen now.

"Steven, come with me. The rest of you stay here. You can all leave except Cindy and Veronica."

When no one moved, he said, "I mean it. Leave now, or I'll arrest you all. Unless someone else wants to confess to the murder of Cedric Jone, and then you can stay."

Judith moved to talk to Booker, and everyone knew he didn't stand a chance. They both stepped out of the room, and when they returned, Booker said, "Okay. Stay. Quietly. Steven, you come with me."

As they left the room, Booker turned back and gave them all the steeliest look he could muster. But he knew it was Judith, not his look, that would keep them quiet.

When they were gone, Judith turned to the group. "If you want to leave, Booker said you can. I'll stay with Cindy and Veronica, and I will let you know what happens."

Everyone glanced at each other and shook their heads. "We stick together," Marsha said. "We'll wait."

• • • ● • ● ● • • •

Booker had put Steven in the interrogation room to give himself some time to think, and went to get them both some coffee.

When the police station was redesigned, they also revamped the appearance of the interrogation room. While it wasn't particularly attractive, it wasn't uninviting either. The people of Spring Falls had agreed that it wasn't necessary to assume everyone brought into that room was a criminal, deserving harsh treatment.

Despite these changes, the room still kept certain features characteristic of an interrogation space. There were no windows, the door could be locked, and a handcuff rail was available if needed. A viewing room was behind a one-way mirror, and a camera recorded everything when necessary, maintaining a balance between a welcoming atmosphere and the practical needs of law enforcement.

Returning with the coffee, Booker found Steven pale and shaking. Steven took the coffee gratefully. He needed something to hold in his hands, something that would give him the courage to continue.

Booker took a sip of coffee and then a deep breath before saying, "You confessed to the murder of Cedric Jacobs. So I have to charge you with the crime and read you your rights."

Steven just nodded, and after Booker finished, Steven said, "Let me make this easy for us both. Yes, I confess to killing Cedric, but it wasn't murder. It was an accident. And I tried to cover it up. That's what I did wrong. I thought I could get away with it, but I just couldn't let either of those two women go to jail for something they didn't do."

"How was it an accident?"

"I frequently provided Cedric with drugs, specifically opioids. He had started taking them years earlier because of a shoulder injury and became addicted. He steered clear of what he called 'hard drugs,' claiming they made him stupid.

"When his doctor refused to prescribe Cedric any more drugs, I stepped in to supply them." He paused, noticing Booker's disapproving expression, and added, "Yes, I knew it was illegal, but he needed them to paint, and I needed to sell his art."

"There was even a suicide note."

"Not really. It was just a note that said, "I'm sorry." He had given that note to me a week before because of a deal that he made without me. He wasn't really sorry, it was just a way he manipulated people. I have a desk drawer full of his apologies. I would bet that both Cindy and Veronica received a few of those notes, too.

"I had stuffed that one into my jacket pocket, and when he collapsed after taking the drugs, I took it out and left it there to make it look like a suicide."

"So you left him there to die because you had supplied the drugs?"

Steven nodded. "And to tell the whole truth, I was glad to see him gone. It seemed like a simple solution. He was a horrible man. I should never have kept representing him. All I felt was relief that I wouldn't have to work with him anymore, and fear that someone would find out that his death was my fault. Which I know makes me a horrible man, too."

"I'll need you to tell me where you got the drugs."

"Yes, whatever you need," Steven said, hoping that Nancy would understand what he had done and not hate him. He knew he was too old to be starting a life with someone. She was too young for him. But he hoped they could be friends. Actually, he hoped that somehow he could be friends with everyone in Spring Falls.

All of that, of course, was now an impossibility, but if he had a chance to make up for what he had done—being a coward, not standing up to Cedric long before—he'd do it. And if that included turning in the people who supplied the drugs to him, he'd do that too.

Although Steven wanted to think that made him a good person, he knew he was eager to help because he wanted to make a bargain to lighten his sentence. Steven was fully aware that he was guilty of many things. He turned a blind eye to Cedric's behavior. He supplied the drugs to Cedric. And he could have carried a Narcan pen, and saved him, and then called for help.

Only a month before, he had learned that he could get Naloxone (Narcan) for free from many community groups in New York city. He had thought of Cedric, and decided not to bother. That made him a bad man, no matter what.

He just hadn't cared enough. Why bother was his motto. He was an art dealer, not a person who meddled with other people's lives. Or helped them, either.

All of that seemed fine until he met the group of friends in Spring Falls, and everything changed. Just a few days with them had opened his eyes. It did matter. He should have cared. He should have helped Cedric. Actually, he should have stopped representing him, and turned him in years before for his behavior with women.

Doing the right thing now would never make up for all that he had done before, but it was a beginning, and maybe he'd discover that part of himself that was still a good person.

Fifty-Five

Judith was doing the same thing that Booker was doing. She was interrogating Cindy and Veronica. She wouldn't call it an interrogation, but it was. At least that's what it felt like to the two of them.

She had pulled up a chair directly in front of them and stared at them until they were both squirming in their seats. Daniel sat behind them with his arm around Emma. Marsha sat on the other side of Emma. She had known that Emma and her mother needed help. But in a million years, she would never have imagined this story.

Bree and April sat in the front row beside Cindy and Veronica. Bree held Cindy's hand and April held Veronica's, both of them thinking that just a few months before, they were the two in trouble.

Judith's hair lit up for a second, and then she took a deep breath and leaned forward. She had been here before. When an accountant or bookkeeper that she hired in her business was accused of doing something wrong, she was never afraid of confronting them. It wouldn't do any good to be nice to them. It solved nothing.

It was kinder to be stern and demand answers. That way, they could all move on. Usually it was a misunderstanding, a secret that hadn't been told, and that was what she thought might come to light here. At least, she hoped it was. But ripping the band-aide off quickly worked best.

"The question is the same for both of you. Why were you in New York? And what happened when you saw Cedric? Who wants to start?"

Veronica and Cindy spoke at the same time. "I didn't see him," and then looked at each other and started laughing.

Even Judith's glare didn't stop them. Soon, the entire room was laughing. It took a few minutes for the laughter to die down, and then Cindy started hiccuping, and they all laughed again.

Finally, Judith managed to quiet the room and, trying once again to be stern, said, "Well, why in the blazes didn't you say that before?"

Once again, Veronica and Cindy said the same thing at the same time. "No one asked."

Judith didn't laugh, and everyone else held back the giggles that threatened to start again. They all knew that the laughter was simply a release of the tension they felt, and eventually, they had to hear the complete story. Because no matter what Steven was saying, he could be lying, and one or both of their friends could be charged with Cedric's death.

"You start, Cindy," Judith said. "Why did you go there? Why didn't you tell anyone? And if you didn't see him, why not?"

"I'm sorry, Judith. I kept the secret of what happened that summer for so long, I couldn't figure out how to tell you. And I had slowly come to understand that it was Cedric who had ruined my ability to paint. He had destroyed my dream because I believed him, and it ruined everything.

"I wanted to confront him, and tell him I knew who he was, and I was going to tell the world. When all those women in the #MeToo movement started speaking up about the men who had used them, I wanted to be like them.

"But when I got to New York, I discovered I was too afraid of him. I was afraid that he would make it even worse by reminding me of what I wasn't. So I stayed one night, and came home. I was so disappointed in myself. It was the last straw. That's what finally brought me to the decision to stop painting all together, and just teach."

Judith didn't waste time in assuring Cindy that what Cedric had told her had been a lie. Her paintings were beautiful. And Cedric had copied them and become a wealthy man. She knew Cindy's life would now be different, but first she had to find out why Veronica had been in New York.

Veronica didn't wait to be asked. "Before my mother died, she told me about my father. She told me about that summer and her friend Cindy."

Turning to Cindy, she said, "But I never put those two things together or thought you were that Cindy. I'm so glad I have met you, though. For years, I wanted to thank you for being so kind to my mom. She kept that note you wrote her."

"I have it now," Emma said. "Mom gave it to me."

Reaching into the case that held her phone, she pulled out the worn piece of paper and read it out loud.

"You are a treasure, my friend. Every day is a gift. Let's always look for its treasures. And in doing so, we will find life's greatest treasure, the gift of giving and receiving love."

Cindy stood and hugged Emma and Veronica. "Linda was an amazing woman. She'd be so proud of you both."

"Despite that," Judith said, "You haven't said what happened in New York."

What Judith was hiding was how hard it was for her not to break down and be part of the hugging that was going on. No, she needed answers, and she needed them before Booker came back into the room to get them.

"Truthfully, nothing happened. I had this idea that I wanted my father to get to know me. It sounds foolish, I know. When I turned eighteen, I began receiving money, and I assumed it was from my father. But couldn't figure out why he sent it.

"I thought my mom might have forced him to provide for me before she passed away. The money wasn't a huge amount, but it was enough to scrape by, and it increased slightly when Emma was born, so I knew someone was keeping tabs on us.

"A few months ago, I decided to confront him. I wanted to ask why he never wanted to meet me or his granddaughter, Emma. I was thankful for the money, but I yearned for him to know Emma and me.

"However, I lost my nerve. I reached New York but turned around and came home without seeing him. When the money stopped coming, I assumed he had discovered my visit to New York, possibly breaching an agreement my mom had made with him to stay away and never reveal our connection.

"It was only later, after learning about his death, that I realized the money would never come again."

Turning in her chair, she held Emma's hands. "I'm sorry for being such a mess for those months. I didn't know what to do."

Booker stood outside the door to the meeting room for a moment, grateful that he had news to share that would relieve everyone in the room. But he couldn't say that he was happy about the outcome. Steven had made some terrible choices, and his choices had resulted in Cedric's death, and Steven would have to pay for what he had done.

Booker knew it was all too easy to make a decision that opened the door to a series of cascading events that would eventually ruin lives. He hoped this was the last time his friends had to face terrible things together, but he doubted that would be true.

Fifty-Six

"We did it," Marsha said to April. They were standing in the middle of the dance studio at the Ruby House, looking out the window at the maple tree, which was now a mass of blazing red and gold leaves.

A long table overflowing with food filled the far end of the room. Silver balloons danced on the ceiling, and live trees in big pots sat in each corner, wearing white sparkle lights. After the party, each of the Ruby Sisters would choose a tree, and a tree service would plant them wherever they wanted them to be.

Marsha thought the trees were a perfect symbol of the life that they shared. She imagined that forever those trees would be aware of each other, just as they were, no matter where they were. It was not only the ruby necklaces that they all wore; it went much deeper than that.

We too have roots that reach towards each other no matter where we are, Marsha thought, wondering if she had ever been this happy before. Everyone and everything was in place. Finally.

Today marked the grand opening of The Ruby House. Given all the trials and tribulations the Ruby Sisters had overcome, the timing couldn't have been better. Every single one of the Ruby Sisters was not just safe, but flourishing in their lives. The moment felt like a long-awaited celebration of their resilience and unity.

Besides, with April soon to embark on an extended trip with Robert, it was essential to hold the grand opening before their departure. Marsha and April had spent many hours discussing April's upcoming absence. Concerns over April's business, along with the operation of the Ruby House, were at the forefront of their conversations.

But when Marsha had reminded her that memories made up life, and it was the perfect time to make new ones with her son, April finally happily gave in. She and Robert would first visit her daughter and her family. Then Robert was taking April on a tour all around Europe. She didn't plan to be back for a few months.

The timing was perfect for April. They had completed the construction of Cindy's art studio. In fact, Cindy had already taught her first art class and declared the space perfect. The Ruby House was complete, and even the police station's construction was also finished. All those projects that had benefited from her thoughtful and unique designs.

"Go now," Marsha had said, "Go while it's quiet, before something else comes up, because with us you know it always does."

From where Marsha and April stood, they could see Robert outside, directing cars into the parking lot. There wouldn't be enough space to park everyone at one time, but it was an open house, not a party, so they expected people to come and go. Besides, much of the town could walk or bike over if they wished to.

It's a good thing that Spring Falls is a small town, Marsha thought, because they had invited everyone, just as Cindy did when she held the art gallery's holiday open house. That always worked well, and Marsha and April hoped the same would be true for them.

They were well prepared. As April said, they had enough food to feed an army, and if they ran out, Robert had reminded them that there was always pizza delivery. The event would go on all day, musicians would take turns playing throughout the day. At the moment, a young woman was playing the harp. Marsha wanted the music to be something that transformed the space, not something that stopped conversation. The harp was perfect.

Marsha had also planned a short recital by the smallest members of the studio. They had been practicing for weeks, but they were so adorable no one would care if they messed up the dance.

While they watched the crowd heading to the house, April and Marsha held hands. They had decided to dress alike, in deep ruby colors. Marsha wore a long, flowing dress, and April had on a pants suit with high-heeled boots. The only jewelry they wore were the ruby necklaces from Harry. They knew every Ruby Sister would wear their necklaces today. After all, this opening resulted from all of their work together.

Robert, too, had on a deep ruby sweater and April thought he looked very handsome. She couldn't wait for their trip to begin. They planned to leave the day after baby Rho's first birthday party that was coming up in a few days.

Marsha and April were watching for four very special people. Nicky had promised to come to the opening, and she was bringing her sister Sara. Although Nicky and Marsha had seen each other often the last few months, their relationship growing stronger each time, Sara had not been back. They were looking forward to showing off all the changes they had made.

They were also looking for Amir, the friend of Marsha's father, Harry. Amir had, with Harry's planning, saved Bree from the fire, and April from being taken away forever by Ron. Amir was bringing his wife.

Marsha couldn't wait to thank her, because while Amir was taking care of her father, Amir had often left his wife and children alone. Now that he was retired, and with the funds her father had left him, she knew they finally had time to enjoy their life together.

"They're here," Marsha whispered to April as the first of the guests walked through the front door.

Marsha bent down to hug April, who looked more like a cardinal today than a wren, before turning to greet their guests, wondering if it was possible to burst open from happiness.

Fifty-Seven

While Daniel waited for Cindy to get ready for the open house, he stood in front of her paintings, captivated by them. He recalled standing in his father's studio just a few months prior, marveling at his father's brilliant artwork despite thinking that he had never known him. How could that horrible man paint those beautiful paintings?

But it turned out he had known his father just fine. Cedric was precisely the man he remembered. However, Daniel's initial impression of the paintings had been spot on, too. They were genuinely captivating and beautiful.

Cindy had given him permission to turn all the paintings away from the wall and to choose the one he wanted for himself. And then to choose the ones that she would hang in her art gallery.

It had taken a little persuasion from everyone, especially Mimi and Janet, to convince Cindy that she not only deserved an art opening of her own, but she had to have one. She agreed with the condition that the proceeds would go to organizations and people who provided safe spaces and counseling for women who had been abused.

It was only after a private gathering of the Ruby Sisters that Cindy had fully accepted that Cedric had abused her. She had known before, but she had kept the realization away from her heart, afraid that it would break her. But the Ruby Sisters reminded her she had to face it in order to let it go. At first, Cindy found it hard to forgive herself for how much she had let it run her life.

She had not been abused the way many women were. But Cedric had colored her life and what she had believed about herself for many years. His form of abuse took away her agency. She acted as if what he told her was real.

"Yes," Marsha had said. "You have lived a good life, but always with that secret buried within you that you weren't good enough. And besides, he told you he was the only one who could help you become at least a decent artist. He held that control over you.

"Perhaps you don't see that as abuse, but it is. And there are many women, and men, who suffer from that kind of abuse. Just think how hard it is for the ones that receive physical abuse to get help. It's obvious what's happening, and still people turn away.

"If you can see what happened to you as abuse, it will help you help others in the same situation."

Cindy was still adjusting to that awareness of what happened to her, but she had decided that after donating all the profit from her art gallery show, she would continue to donate a percentage of all her art sales towards helping other victims of abuse. The first showing at her art gallery would be just the beginning.

A few nights later, she had shared with Daniel that she realized that because of what had happened with Cedric, it was probably why she was never able to settle down with anyone.

"And you'll settle down with me?" Daniel had asked.

Cindy's answer was a simple, "Yes."

What that meant, neither of them knew. They both understood that they had things to work out. But as far as Daniel was concerned, he'd wait forever for her. After all, he had been ten years old when he first fell in love with her. He could wait a few more years if necessary.

He was still trying to decide which painting he wanted when Cindy asked from the doorway, "Have you chosen the one you want?"

Daniel turned to see Cindy in a dress that shimmered from blue to purple, her ruby necklace glittering in the light, and decided that she looked just like her paintings. Joyous, beautiful, with a depth that meant you had to look at them over and over again just to get a glimpse of the meaning.

"I did," he said, leaning over to kiss her. "I choose the artist."

Fifty-Eight

Judith and Bruce were in her garden. Booker and Bree had just left.

The couple had stopped by after the open house to update them on the aftermath of Steven's arrest for criminally negligent homicide. Steven had, after all, supplied Cedric with the fatal drug, failed to seek emergency assistance, and attempted to conceal his involvement.

Yet, even with these charges, Steven wouldn't be serving jail time. Thanks to his proficient lawyer, he received a lighter sentence consisting of a five-year probation period, a monetary fine, and a requirement to commit to volunteer work during his probationary period.

After much discussion, Cindy agreed to have Steven manage the sale of her paintings. Despite initially mistaking them for Cedric's work, he had developed a profound understanding of Cindy's art. Besides, he was Daniel's friend too, and like all of them, he deserved a second chance.

It was a warm October evening, something to be treasured while they could. Winter would be here soon, which had its own charm.

Judith had hugged Booker and Bree goodbye and then sat back in her chair with a sigh.

"Something bothering you, Judith?" Bruce asked.

It had been a wonderful day. The open house had gone smoothly. Not just smoothly, perfectly. Even the children's dance had gone off without a hitch.

Judith had worked the room while Bruce watched, thinking how lucky he was that she had chosen him. He admired her people skills. Despite often being the one who called attention to what was wrong, somehow she managed to not offend people.

To anyone else, Judith looked calm and assured. But for the past few weeks, he had sensed something else. But he had not asked because helping Cindy and Veronica came first. However, now that everything had settled down, he knew it was time to find out what was on her mind.

At first he had been worried that her upset had to do with him. But every time she looked at him, he saw the truth. It wasn't him. Bruce knew she was a little worried about Nancy. Nancy had seen the good in Steven, and was understandably upset when she learned what he had done.

When Judith told her she could take time off, Nancy had said she had been wrong about people before, and would be again, let her work. Besides, Steven could turn himself into a better man, so she'd wait and see. Judith seemed pleased with Nancy's decision, so he didn't think it had to do with her.

So what was it? Bruce knew that Bree had sensed something too, and if Judith didn't tell him what was going on, he'd ask Bree to help him uncover what was bothering her.

Whatever it was, Bruce knew he would be there for her.

So he asked again, "I know something is bothering you, Judith. Tell me, we'll work it out together."

Judith put her coffee down, looked up at the clear sky, and sighed, before turning to answer him.

She wanted to say that nothing was wrong. But something was. She felt it. Her hair tingled when she thought of it. She had lain awake nights wondering what to do. If she told Bruce, what could he do? She wasn't sure what she could do about it herself.

She had told herself it was the way of the world. Leave it alone. But that wasn't in her nature. Eventually, she'd have to tell someone. But was that tonight?

"Something is going on, Bruce. Or at least I think something is. And if I am right, the whole town is in danger."

"Then let's not talk about it tonight. Let's stay in the celebration of today. And tomorrow, you can tell me."

Judith nodded yes, leaned back in her chair to stare at the beautiful clear sky, full of stars, grateful that she had time to think about what she knew, and perhaps find out that she was wrong.

The trouble was, she didn't think so.

Author Note

Throughout my life—whether in the role of choreographer, financial planner, friend, or coach—I have noticed how often we believe something told to us, and it changes the course of our lives.

Too often, that belief keeps us from doing what our heart desires. We stop believing we have a gift to be shared with the world, or that we have a right to share it.

Dolly Parton's saying, "Find out who you are and do it on purpose" comes to the heart of it.

But when someone has told us we aren't worth it, or good enough, how do we overcome it?

And just like Cindy in this book, too often we keep that to ourselves, and just give up.

Yes, I know. We are not all good at everything. But when we deny the gift that we have been given, and give up, it's a tragedy. Not just for us, but for everyone else we would serve by sharing our gift.

Does it matter if it's one person or thousands that we share it with? No. Only that we express it.

So if you are hiding a desire to do something, and you believe that you can't do it, or are not capable, or not allowed, please look again at where that belief comes from. As Byron Katie says, "Ask yourself, is that true?"

Be honest. If you are not sure, ask someone who has your best interests in mind.

My guess is that you are good enough at what you desire to do, because like the desire of the acorn to become a tree, it is innately you.

As Cindy said in this book, "You are a treasure, my friend. Every day is a gift. Let's always look for its treasures. And in doing so, we will find life's greatest treasure, the gift of giving and receiving love."

~Beca

The next book, in this series, *Almost Innocent*, features Judith. What is going on in Spring Falls that we haven't seen before? Find the answer in this next book in the Ruby Sister's series.

PS:

Did you like visiting Grace and her friend in Doveland? You can read more about Grace and her friends in the Doveland Series. The story begins in Doveland with *Pragma*

Acknowledgements

I could never write a book without the help of my friends and my book community. When people ask me, where's the next book, I feel a rush of excitement to get it done—just for them.

Thank you, Jet Tucker, Jamie Lewis, and Diana Cormier for taking the time to do the final reader proof. You are a loyal and much-loved reader team. You can't imagine how much I appreciate it.

And a massive final thank you to Barbara Budan, who has left this plane of existence. But wherever she is, I am sure she is extending help to anyone that needs it. I will sorely miss Barbara's notes to me after each book, always finding something the rest of us didn't see. Someday we will meet again.

And as always, thank you to Laura Moliter for her fantastic book editing.

Thank you to every other member of my Book Community who helps me make so many decisions that help the book be the best book possible.

Thank you to all the people who tell me they love to read these stories. Those random comments from friends and strangers are more valuable than gold.

And as always, thank you to my beloved husband, Del, for being my daily sounding board, for putting up with all my questions, my constant need to want to make things better, and for being the love of my life, in more than just this one lifetime.

Connect with me online:

Facebook: https://www.facebook.com/becalewiscreative
Instagram: https://instagram.com/becalewis
TikTok: https://tiktok.com/@becalewis
Twitter: http://twitter.com/becalewis
LinkedIn: https://linkedin.com/in/becalewis
Youtube: https://www.youtube.com/c/becalewis

Also By Beca

The Ruby Sisters Series: Women's Lit, Friendship
A Last Gift, After All This Time, And Then She Remembered, As If It Was Real, Almost Innocent

Stories From Doveland: Magical Realism, Friendship
Karass, Pragma, Jatismar, Exousia, Stemma, Paragnosis, In-Between, Missing, Out Of Nowhere

The Return To Erda Series: Fantasy
Shatterskin, Deadsweep, Abbadon, The Experiment

The Chronicles of Thamon: Fantasy
Banished, Betrayed, Discovered, Wren's Story

The Shift Series: Spiritual Self-Help
Living in Grace: The Shift to Spiritual Perception
The Daily Shift: Daily Lessons From Love To Money
The 4 Essential Questions: Choosing Spiritually Healthy Habits
The 28 Day Shift To Wealth: A Daily Prosperity Plan

The Intent Course: Say Yes To What Moves You
Imagination Mastery: A Workbook For Shifting Your Reality
Right Thinking: A Thoughtful System for Healing
Perception Mastery: Seven Steps To Lasting Change
Blooming Your Life: How To Experience Consistent Happiness

Perception Parables: Very short stories
Love's Silent Sweet Secret: A Fable About Love
Golden Chains And Silver Cords: A Fable About Letting Go

Advice:
A Woman's ABC's of Life: Lessons in Love, Life, and Career from Those Who Learned The Hard Way
The Daily Nudge(s): So When Did You First Notice

About Beca

Beca writes books she hopes will change people's perceptions of themselves and the world, and open possibilities to things and ideas that are waiting to be seen and experienced.

At sixteen, Beca founded her own dance studio. Later, she received a Master's Degree in Dance in Choreography from UCLA and founded the Harbinger Dance Theatre, a multimedia dance company, while continuing to run her dance school.

After graduating—to better support her three children—Beca switched to the sales field, where she worked as an employee and independent contractor to many industries, excelling in each while perfecting and teaching her Shift System® and writing books.

She joined the financial industry in 1983 and became an Associate Vice President of Investments at a major stock brokerage firm, and was a licensed Certified Financial Planner for over twenty years.

This diversity, along with a variety of life challenges, helped fuel the desire to share what she's learned by writing and speaking, hoping it will make a difference in other people's lives.

Beca grew up in State College, PA, with the dream of becoming a dancer and then a writer. She carried that dream forward as she fulfilled a childhood wish by moving to Southern California in 1968. Beca told her family she would never move back to the cold.

After living there for thirty-one years, she met her husband Delbert Lee Piper, Sr., at a retreat in Virginia, and everything changed. They decided to find a place they could call their own, which sent them off traveling around the United States. They lived and worked in a few different places before returning to live in the cold once again near Del's family in a small town in Northeast Ohio, not too far from State College.

When not working and teaching together, they love to visit and play with their combined family of eight children and five grandchildren, read, study, do yoga or taiji, feed birds, and work in their garden.

Printed by Amazon Italia Logistica S.r.l.
Torrazza Piemonte (TO), Italy